Stealing
Popular

GET IN THE M!X!
HAVE YOU READ ALL THE M!X BOOKS?

Stealing Popular

TRUDI TRUEIT

ALADDIN MIX
New York London Toronto Sydney New Delhi

ALADDIN M!X
Simon & Schuster Children's Publishing Division
1230 Avenue of the Americas, New York, NY 10020
First Aladdin M!X edition September 2012
Copyright © 2012 by Trudi Strain Trueit
All rights reserved, including the right of reproduction
in whole or in part in any form.
ALADDIN is a trademark of Simon & Schuster, Inc., and related logo
is a registered trademark of Simon & Schuster, Inc.
ALADDIN M!X and related logo are registered trademarks of Simon & Schuster, Inc.
For information about special discounts for bulk purchases, please contact
Simon & Schuster Special Sales at 1-866-506-1949
or business@simonandschuster.com.
The Simon & Schuster Speakers Bureau can bring authors to your
live event. For more information or to book an event contact the
Simon & Schuster Speakers Bureau at 1-866-248-3049 or
visit our website at www.simonspeakers.com.
Designed by Karina Granda
The text of this book was set in Hoefler Text.
Manufactured in the United States of America 0812 OFF
2 4 6 8 10 9 7 5 3 1
Library of Congress Control Number 2012936751
ISBN 978-1-4424-4154-5
ISBN 978-1-4424-4155-2 (eBook)

This book is for every Nobody,
who has yet to discover
the Somebody within.

Acknowledgments

With love to my niece, Trina Lee, whose creative and compassionate spirit inspired my heroine. With deepest thanks to Liesa Abrams and Alyson Heller, my editors, and to Rosemary Stimola, my agent—three of the most gifted and giving women I know. And to William, with all my heart, who writes a delightful new chapter in our love story every day.

Destiny is not a matter of chance,
it is a matter of choice;
it is not a thing to be waited for,
it is a thing to be achieved.

—William Jennings Bryan

One

By the time I got to Briar Green Middle School in the spring of seventh grade, I was a master magician.

I could create a force field around me strong enough to deflect the meanest insult. I could make it rain silver glitter each time a teacher mispronounced, misspelled, or forgot my name. But my greatest trick? I could dissolve into mist the moment a popular person entered the room.

Poof!

That's what happens when you go to five schools in seven years. You create illusions. It's how you survive. My magic was working perfectly, too, until the first day of eighth grade.

That's the day I began to reappear.

It happened in D wing in front of an ordinary, orange corner locker with a boomerang-shaped dent and a blue dragonfly sticker. The locker wasn't even mine. It was

Fawn's—well, the one she was *supposed* to have.

At Briar Green Middle School we're assigned lockers based on gender and alphabetical last name. You are not supposed to trade, move in with someone else, or be reassigned, even if your locker isn't in the same galaxy as any of your classes. I have no idea why. It's a rule, and rules are sacred here, including the dumb ones. You'd think the way Mrs. Gisborne, our head counselor, freaks out, one little locker swap is going to create a black hole that will suck Briar Green Middle School (a.k.a. BGMS) into a massive vortex of death. Yes, I am aware of my school's unfortunate initials. Our mascot is the St. Bernard, which, unfortunately, makes me a Big Mess St. Bernard.

Fawn's last name is Ralston, so, naturally, when assigning lockers for the new school year, the computer paired her up with the next girl on the list: Dijon Randle. Now, *there* was a big mess. Dijon and her friends—Venice Wasserman, Truffle Tompkins, and Évian James—were royalty. Seriously. Every Friday they wore fake diamond tiaras to school. Big Mess—with its peeling orange walls, leaky ceilings, and dead plants in the courtyard— was their kingdom. The Royal Court would happily tell you what to think and what to say, how to act and how to dress, whom to love and whom to hate—all for a Starbucks gift card. And your soul.

Not that I let it get to me. Bossy girls existed at every school I'd ever been to. My parents are divorced, and my dad's in the navy, so we move a lot. I live with my dad at the Eagle's Nest apartments (no one seems to know why there's a seagull on the sign out front).

It didn't take me long to figure out how things worked at Big Mess: Any girl named after a gourmet food, fancy water, or a city was a Somebody. Top athletes and elected student leaders were Sortabodies. Everybody else was a Nobody. Somebodies could associate with Sortabodies, but only in public and for no longer than ten minutes. Sortabodies could talk to Nobodies, but could not eat, study, or become friends with them for fear of being seen by a Somebody and being demoted to a Nobody. Nobodies were not allowed within a five-foot radius of a Somebody, unless verbally invited into the inner circle by the aforementioned Somebody. In the case of Dijon, which was both a gourmet food *and* a city, verbal permission and a gift card were required.

I was a Nobody (surprise!). So were my friends, Fawn Ralston and Adair Clarke. It *feels* weird saying that. I'd never had any actual friends before I came to Big Mess (not counting my hamster, Dash). If you're a kid, the military pretty much torpedoes your social life. At my other schools I *knew of* people. And people *knew of* me. I was the girl who always had her head in her sketchbook, doodling pictures she never showed to anyone. But no one ever really got to *know* me. And I never really got to *know* anyone. I suppose it was mostly my fault I was a "knew of" girl and not a "get to know" girl. When you moved as much as I did, it was easier to remain alone than to be forever saying good-bye. That's what you tell yourself, anyway. But it's an illusion, too. Truth was, I hadn't ever had anybody to say good-bye to. All that changed when I came to Big Mess—and on my very first day. I met Fawn and Adair within a half hour of being on campus. They'd come to my rescue. I was standing in the courtyard (the one with the dead plants), trying not to look like I was totally lost, though I *was* totally lost.

"You're looking for Portable Thirteen, aren't you?"

"How did . . . ?"

"Because nobody is ever *that* interested in the shriveled-up junipers." A tall, athletic girl wearing a sunflower-print skirt grinned. "I'm Adair Clarke." Her blond ponytail swung as she dipped her head toward the petite, dark-haired girl beside her. "This is Fawn Ralston."

Fawn, wearing a white lace turtleneck under a vest that could have doubled as a chessboard, lifted a sleeve and waved. "Hi." She said it so softly, I had to lip-read.

"I'm Coco Sherwood," I said, activating my emergency force field. People do one of two things when they hear my name: They either frown and say, "How strange," or they smile and ask, "Is your middle name Puffs?"

Get it? Cocoa Puffs?

So pathetic.

I always answer, "Actually, it's Krispies." I say it with a straight face, so they aren't sure if I am joking or not. My middle name is really Simone, after my mother, but I've got to have *some* fun.

I was ready for either response when Fawn said, "Cool! I love fashion, and your name is the same as one of my favorite designers. Have you ever heard of Coco Chanel?"

I was going to say she sounded familiar, but Adair never gave me the chance. "Wow!" she burst. "You're also named after my favorite drink, hot cocoa with mini-marshmallows."

Fawn gasped. "Adair!"

"What'd I say?"

"That's rude. She's not a drink."

"Who wouldn't want to be a drink? You can call me Oreo Milk Shake any time you want!"

We laughed and started talking about our favorite beverages. Mine is raspberry lemonade (heavy on the lemon). Love, love, *love* it!

I soon discovered I had the same science class as Adair, which turned out to be in Portable 13 (unmarked, of course), located behind a lawn-mower shed across from the giant trash bins at the far end of campus. We couldn't help but wonder what *that* teacher did to end up in middle-school Siberia!

Anyway, you can imagine the ugly scene Dijon made when she discovered she got my friend—soft-spoken, quirky dresser, Nobody Fawn Ralston—for a locker partner. I don't have to imagine anything. I was there.

See, your red locker-assignment card doesn't reveal who your partner is going to be. You get the thrill of discovering that all by yourself. The administration thinks we like surprises. We don't. Middle school is full of surprises. They are rarely good. We get stuff like volcanic zits that choose picture day to explode on our chins and the cafeteria's scalding chicken noodle soup (which has neither chicken nor noodles, but does, strangely, have beans).

So this is how it went down. Fawn and I were walking through the hall on the second floor of D wing, scanning the row of lockers to find the number on her card: 229. Dijon, Évian, Truffle, and Venice were doing the same thing, only coming from the other direction. Guess where we all met? Worse, Fawn and Dijon reached for the exact same metal knob at the exact same time. Their fingers touched. The earth trembled (well, not really, but Venice and Truffle screamed and clung to each other as if we were having a 9.5 quake). Not only had we violated the five-foot-radius rule, but a Nobody had actually *touched* a Somebody. That was strictly forbidden and was punishable by Dijon's nanny running over you in a midnight blue Ferrari.

"What do you think you're doing?" barked Dijon.

"Uh . . . I . . ." Fawn tugged on the frilly sleeve of her poet blouse. Fawn was shy around the Somebodies, but her retro fashions and the magenta stripe on the side of her angled, chin-length bob said everything she could not. Fawn, unable to come up with anything resembling a word, held out her locker card.

"Oh, bloody warts. You?" Dijon made a face. "I got *you*?"

My body stiffened.

"Megacatastrophe," said Venice, chomping her gum. Venice always had gum. You could hear her chewing from across the quad. *Snap. Snap. Snap.* It sounded like bacon frying. "What are you going to do, Dij?"

Dijon shot her an irritated glance over her shoulder, as if to say, *Me? I'm not going to do anything.* Two turquoise fingernails carefully lined up the number thirteen to the red vertical line, then spun the dial to the left. The three of us watched as she lined up the number twenty-two, then flung the dial right. Dijon cupped her left hand around the knob so we couldn't see the last number. Hello? Didn't Her Fabulousness realize Fawn had the very same locker combination in her hand? That was my nickname for Dijon: Her Fabulousness. It was Dijon's favorite word. Everything was "fabulous this," and "fabulous that," and "Aren't I the most fabulous person ever?"

Dijon lifted the handle and opened the locker. We all gaped, as if expecting to see stacks of gold bars or piles of jewels or something befitting Her Fabulousness. The locker was empty. Dijon hung her mocha leather backpack embossed with the initials DAR on one side of the two-pronged center hook. When Fawn started to put her orange-and-red-striped nylon pack on the other side, Dijon's arm shot out to block her. "What are you doing?"

"Hanging up my—"

"You are not my locker partner. I am not your locker partner. We're not ever going to *be* locker partners."

A warm tingle crept up my neck.

"But my card says—"

"It's a mistake, obviously."

"Obviously," echoed Venice, pausing her chompfest to let out a cackle. Venice was Dijon's first runner-up. You know, in the event Dijon couldn't fulfill her duties as queen (say, she got pushed off a thousand-foot cliff by a member of the Royal Court), Venice would be promoted to Her Fabulousness. Venice tapped the pointed toe of her gray leather, knee-high boot. "You'll have to go get another one."

"Another locker?" Two pink splotches appeared on Fawn's cheeks. "But . . . Mrs. Gisborne won't let us . . . I . . . I guess I could ask. Maybe, just for now, I could leave my stuff here and—"

"No," said Dijon.

"No," echoed Venice.

"But I—"

"Are you deaf?" Truffle snapped, punching Fawn in the shoulder.

"Whoa!"

Had I said that? I must have, because everyone was staring at me. Clearly, I was no longer mist. I was real. And here. And angry.

"It's her assigned locker," I said, my fingers tightening around my sketchbook. "Where is she supposed to put her stuff?"

Dijon inspected my jeans, my white T-shirt with its stamped red swirl print, and my red hoodie to confirm my Nobodiness. She leaned toward me. "Anywhere but here." Her words froze into crystals the moment they hit air. I felt the chill. Dijon slammed the locker door. The sound ricocheted through my head. She calmly spun the dial, then strolled back down the way she had come. As the Royal Court hurried to catch up to her, their heels went *clitter-clap*, *clitter-clap* against the white-and-green-speckled tiles.

"Do you think she'll put up her beauty board again?" asked Fawn, rubbing her shoulder.

"Yep," I answered quickly.

Last year Dijon had hung a heart-shaped dry-erase board on the outside of her locker. On it she'd written weekly makeup tips and commands for her royal subjects. She'd scribbled things like, "Wear red on Monday" or "Buy Taffy Joy eye shadow #33." I confess, like most every girl at Big Mess, I read the board. However, unlike most every girl at Big Mess, I refused to obey it. At that moment I swore an oath to never again so much as glance at Dijon Randle's beauty board.

"Come on," I said, picking up Fawn's orange backpack by the top loop. "You can share my locker."

"Don't you have a partner?"

I did. We'd only just met, though her name was familiar. I think we'd had a class together last spring. I didn't know much about her other than she was a Nobody, like me. And she looked like Tinker Bell. Without the gossamer wings and wand, of course.

"Liezel won't mind," I said.

"Liezel? Liezel Sheppard is your locker partner?"

"Uh-huh."

Fawn's lips turned up. "No, she wouldn't mind." The grin faded. "But the rule—"

"Is dumb."

"If Mrs. Gisborne finds out, you'll get in trouble."

I lifted my chin. "I live for trouble."

Fawn groaned, because we both knew that was a humpback whale of a lie. We were Nobodies, and Nobodies always followed the rules—everybody's rules. We hated it. But we did it.

Watching Her Fabulousness and the Royal Court glide away, their grand parade interrupted with a nod to a Sortabody and a faux greeting to a teacher, I began to peel the blue dragonfly sticker off locker 229. Venice and Truffle kept stealing glances at us and trading whispers. Dijon, however, didn't look back. Not once. She merely continued on her way, having all but forgotten our minor intrusion into her glamorous, fabulous world.

I wondered: How had Her Fabulousness and the Royal Court gotten so much power? Had anyone ever defied them? Was it even possible? I didn't have any answers, but wondering, as anybody who's a Nobody will tell you, can lead to all kinds of dangerous thoughts.

Two

With the handing out of class schedules, seasonal joy spread far and wide throughout the kingdom of Big Mess.

Not.

Aunt Iona, my dad's sister, says I can be a little sarcastic.

Nah. I can be *a lot* sarcastic.

I don't know how Fawn and I managed to find Adair in the huge crowd of seventh and eighth graders waiting to get into the gym (sixth graders reported to the cafeteria). But we did. Good thing, too. When the doors opened, the three of us were swept inside along with the wave of bodies. Once in the foyer, I could see through the next set of double doors that the big dividers had been pulled across the center of the gym.

"Seventh grade to the left. Eighth grade to the right!"

shouted Mr. Falkner, our assistant principal. "Parker Silberhagen, what grade are you in?"

"Uh, eighth?"

It was a mystery how he'd gotten that far. The kid had to have help to turn on his phone.

"So where should you be going?"

"Left?"

Mr. Falkner smacked his palm against his forehead. "Try the other left, Parker. Seventh grade to the left, please. Eighth grade to the right. Keep it moving, people."

Something sharp dug into my spine. "Ouch!" I tried to look back to see what it was, but there were too many people. I was being propelled by the crowd behind me.

"Hold on to me," said Adair, hooking her elbow through mine.

"Where's your sketchbook?" a worried Fawn shouted from the other side of Adair. I pointed to my backpack.

We found seats in the middle section of the bleachers about halfway up. Her Fabulousness and the Royal Court sat several rows down, close to the main floor. Dijon swung around. Judgmental eyes began scanning the bleachers.

I closed my eyes. *I am mist. I am mist. I am mist.*

When I opened them, Dijon was looking at me. So much for magic. Had I forgotten? Or was it gone for good?

I shrank down behind a tall kid in front of me until Dijon turned around.

From the top of the bleachers Parker and his friends, Todd Pishke and Breck Hanover, kept throwing stuff at us.

"Ow." Fawn reached for the back of her head. "Was that a pebble?"

"Whopper," I said, kicking the malt ball through the space in the bleachers beneath us.

"Don't look around. It'll only encourage them," said Adair, pulling her hair back into a ponytail. Adair's long, straight hair was the color of fresh corn on the cob. She looked like she ought to be skipping through a meadow in slow motion for a country music video, but she was so much fun, you forgot to be depressed that she was so gorgeous and you were so . . .

Not.

When the bell finally rang, we had a pep talk from our principal, Dr. Philemina Adams. She said something about this being the best year ever and how proud she was that we were all filled to the brim with St. Bernard spit. She might have said St. Bernard *spirit*. That makes more sense, doesn't it? Adair, Fawn, and I were too busy whispering to pay attention.

"We'd all better have, at least, two classes together," hissed Adair.

Fawn and I agreed. Two was our absolute minimum. Last spring I had three classes with Adair and four with Fawn. It was perfect! As Dr. Adams's short pep talk got longer and longer, we began to get restless.

"Do you think she'll finish before lunch?" asked Adair, taking off her denim jacket.

"Not at this rate," I moaned. I dug out my leather-bound sketchbook from my backpack. I unzipped it, found a fresh page, and started drawing Fawn's profile.

Out of the corner of my eye I watched Adair turn the sleeve of her jacket inside out. She smoothed it out on her lap, then popped the cap off a black permanent marker.

"What are you doing?" I asked.

"Writing my locker combo on the inside of my sleeve," she said, the cap now between her teeth. "It takes me forever to learn it. This way, I don't have to ever worry about forgetting it."

"Do you think that's such a good idea?"

"Nobody can see it here. Plus, it's better than looking like a dork digging out my stupid locker card."

She had a point.

"My lips are so dry, they're about to fall off," said Fawn. "Does anybody have any lip balm?"

"Nope," I said. "Hold still. I am doing your nose."

"Fix the awful dent on the side, please."

"What do I look like, Photoshop? Besides, it's cute. It makes you *you*."

"I have plenty of me. I want killer beauty."

I shook my head. Fawn didn't need my help. She *was* beautiful. Doelike eyes. Pale freckle-free, flawless skin. Delicate nose (with a barely noticeable dimple, not some hideous deformity, as she kept insisting). How could she not see it?

"I might have some lip balm," said Adair, sliding her arms into her jacket. She reached down for her purse.

"It's not a Rebel kind, is it?" asked Fawn.

"No one in their right mind would buy that goo."

I grunted. "Oh yeah? My aunt gave me a whole set of Rebel lip gloss for Christmas last year."

"Ew," Fawn and Adair said together.

"Did you try all of the flavors?"

"I had to. She kept asking me about them. Movie

17

Madness was okay. It's a weird, rusty shade of brown, but it tastes good—like caramel corn."

"Cadence says there's one that tastes like a corn dog," said Fawn.

"That's Baseball Fever," I said, using the side of the sharpened pencil to shade Fawn's nose. "The flavor isn't bad, but you look like you have mustard on your lips."

They squealed.

"That's not the worst one."

"What could be more horrible than mustard lips?" giggled Fawn.

"Glow-in-the-dark lips," I shot back. "We're talking neon yellow here. It's called Firefly. It tastes like onions."

"Ick to the hundredth power." Adair zipped the top of her purse. "Sorry, Fawn. I must have left it in my PE locker."

Fawn let out a groan. To get the lip balm, she'd have to get past the office in the locker room shared by Mrs. Notting and Miss Furdy, our PE teachers. They were strict. Not normal strict. Crazy strict. Whenever you made the slightest mistake, Mrs. Notting would put a check mark next to your name on her enormous aluminum clipboard. To the PE teachers, your worth as

a human being was determined by your athletic ability. If you couldn't (or wouldn't) stop a soccer ball with
your face, you were swiping perfectly good oxygen
from those who could (or would). At my other schools I
played basketball and usually got As in PE, but because
I wasn't on a Big Mess sports team, I didn't count. It
didn't matter that I started at Big Mess *after* basketball
season ended.

Dr. Adams was wrapping up her rah-rah speech.
Finally! We clapped for her as she left the gym, wondering if we would ever see her the rest of the semester. Principals spend a lot of time in meetings. Or so they tell you.
Personally, I think they ditch us to go eat hot wings with
the other middle-school principals at Grillin' Gil's BBQ
Barn on Route 4. I know that's what *I'd* do.

"Don't forget the plan," whispered Adair.

Step one: We were to text one another during the
break after first period to verify we all had the same
lunch. Eating together was nonnegotiable. When you're
a Nobody, it's all you've got. Step two: We were to meet
in the hall outside the cafeteria as soon as possible after
third period (or fourth, depending on which lunch
we had), so we could proceed to step three: claiming
our lunch table. Choosing a table was critical because

whatever you got on that first day of school, you'd be stuck with for the rest of the year. It was a delicate process. You didn't want to be within Tater-Tots-tossing range of the Somebodies, but you also didn't want to be in the boonies where you'd have to humor Mr. Quigley, our lunchroom monitor. He had a foldout wallet with 187 pictures of his tuxedo cat, Clawed Monet.

"What if we don't have any classes together?" gulped Fawn. "What if we don't even have lunch together?"

"We can't think that way," I said, closing my sketchbook. "Positive thoughts, everybody."

"Positive thoughts," affirmed my two best friends.

What else could we do? We were three Nobodies treading water in the vast, stormy ocean of middle school. The best we could do was hold on to one another, kick like mad, and pray for a miracle. If the sharks got us, well, they got us.

Wearing a prune-colored polyester pantsuit and matching low-heeled pumps, Mrs. Gisborne clomped across the gym floor. Her chubby hands reached to turn on the microphone.

In a voice thinner than a tulip petal, Fawn said, "Here we go."

Three

"Waffles is crooked again," said Adair.

Nobody knew for sure why Mrs. Gisborne wore a poofy wiglet on top of her head. She had plenty of hair. Her wiglet looked like something you'd pull out of your shower drain. People were forever gossiping about it. Some kids said it was to cover a stress-related, eighth-grader-induced bald spot. Dewey Parnell said she was using it to smuggle sticky notes and other office supplies home. But I doubted that. Mrs. Gisborne was too nice for that. We named it Waffles. The wiglet, I mean. Adair once said the big tuft of hair reminded her of her grandma's dog, Waffles, and it stuck. Today Waffles was attached to Mrs. Gisborne's scalp with three pastel pink butterfly hair clips. Each butterfly had two long, bouncy, metal antennae.

"Once you receive your schedule, you must immediately exit the gym and report to your first-period class," said Mrs. Gisborne, her butterfly antennae waving at us. "No dilly-dallying. No waiting for your friends. No stopping at your locker."

It looked like Fawn wasn't going to be able to get Adair's lip balm, after all.

While another counselor, Mr. Rottle, stood nearby to hand out the schedule cards, Mrs. Gisborne began reading the names from her alphabetized list. "Abbott, James. Ackerman, Shaelynn. Adler, Kendra . . ."

I felt a bonk on the back of my head. Despite Adair's advice, I had to swing around. At the top of the bleachers Todd and Parker were snickering. A grinning Breck made his eyebrows dance. I pulled my hood over my left shoulder, fished out the Whopper trapped inside, and popped the malt ball into my mouth.

Take that, boys!

Soon Mrs. Gisborne called, "Clarke, Adair."

Adair squished past us to reach the aisle. "Stay strong. Text you soon."

Fawn, being an *R*, was the next to go. When her name was called, she gave me a weak smile, tucked her magenta streak behind her ear, and got up. Something fell to the floor. I reached down. It was Fawn's locker assignment card. I called out to her, but she was already halfway down the steps. I tucked the card inside my backpack to give to her later.

On her way out Dijon did a ballerina twirl to a hearty round of applause. I threw my hoodie over my head and tried not to hurl my oatmeal. It wasn't long before Mrs. Gisborne hit the *S*s.

"Sheppard, Liezelotta."

"Liezelotta?" screamed Venice, poking Truffle next to her. "No wonder she goes by Liezel."

Truffle shouted, "Liezelotta has gotta lotta name!"

The bleachers erupted in laughter. I didn't see what was so funny. But with Dijon and Évian now gone, apparently it was left to Venice and Truffle to rip into the Nobodies.

I felt a breeze and glanced up to see my new locker partner trotting down the steps. Knowing it was almost my turn, I stood up, which is how I got a clear view of a gray leather, knee-high boot shooting out into the middle of the aisle. Suddenly Liezel Sheppard was airborne. Her backpack sailed left. Her purse veered right. And Liezel soared straight—for about two seconds. Then gravity won.

Boom!

The crash shook the gym. It was followed by a chorus of "Ooohs!"

Sprawled facedown on the hardwood, Liezel's right arm was flung out to the side, her left arm was bent under her body, and her legs—oh, her legs—were in an awkward wishbone position.

Miss Aquino, a teacher's aide, and Vice Principal Falkner rushed to Liezel's side.

Venice and Truffle were howling.

Go ahead and laugh, girls, 'cause you're about to get in some serious trouble. Have fun with Mrs. Pescatori in the detention room.

Mrs. Pescatori had been a detention lady with the Oak Harbor school district since 1967. Anybody sent to the Big Mess detention room in the basement was forced to knit booties for her bulldogs, Winston Churchill and General MacArthur. If you didn't know how to knit, you learned. Fast.

I folded my arms and waited for the vice principal or one of the counselors to walk over and march the girls down to the office for their punishment. But that wasn't what happened.

What *did* happen?

"Sherman, Kayla. Sherman, Richard. Sherrill, Thomas."

That's right—nothing.

Not. One. Thing.

Mrs. Gisborne's butterflies were boinging again, and Mr. Rottle was straightening his stack of schedule cards. The girls in the Royal Court were still laughing. Could it be that everybody, including the handful of adults in the gym, thought Liezel's fall was an accident? I couldn't be the *only* person to know the truth, could I? Other kids had to have seen it too. I glanced around quickly, but I was the only one standing up. Nobody was going to say anything. Nobody was going to defy the Royal Court. I should have known. It's how things were done at Big Mess. It was how they would always be done. And honestly? It made me mad.

I raced down the stairs and knelt by a red-faced Liezel. Pale green eyes with specks of gold were fighting back tears. Liezel was trying to wriggle out of Miss Aquino's grasp, desperate to put the disaster behind her.

"Does this hurt?" said Miss Aquino, gently probing Liezel's elbow.

"No," she croaked. "I'm all right. Really, Miss A."

"If it starts to hurt—"

"I'll go to the nurse's office right away, I promise," said Liezel, scrambling for her books. "Coco, could you . . . ?"

"I'll get your purse." I went for the light pink leather hobo bag lying a few feet away. Dropping a silver barrette, a pen, and a tube of clear lip gloss into the purse, I handed it back to her.

"Thanks," she said, wiping away a tear before it could slip down her cheek.

"I saw what happened," I said softly.

Glassy, pale green eyes met mine. Liezel lifted her hand, but she was too late to stop a second tear from falling. My heart hurt for her. She didn't deserve what Venice had done to her. She didn't deserve that kind of embarrassment. Nobody did.

"Sherwood, Coco." Mrs. Gisborne accidentally mispronounced my name as "Caw-coe." If anybody laughed, I didn't hear it. Was that a drizzle of silver glitter I felt on my forehead? It was good to know I still had a bit of magic left.

There was a clear CD jewel case near my foot. I picked it up. "Is this yours too? There's a crack in the corner, but I think the disc is okay."

"I don't want to lose that," said Liezel. "It's my band."

I read the handwritten label on the disc: *Avalanche*. I'd never heard of it. "This is your favorite band?"

"No, it's *my* band. I play guitar in a rock group."

"Really?" I could see pixielike Liezel playing in a chamber music quartet, but a rock band?

"It's my cousin's band, actually. He goes to Oak Harbor High."

"Could I listen to it?"

"Sure. Just leave it in our locker when you're done."

"Hey, Weasel and Cuckoo, hurry up, will you?" called Truffle. "You're holding everybody up."

"Weasel and Cuckoo," cried Venice. "That sounds like a good title for a children's book. *Weasel and Cuckoo Fall on Their Butts!*" She let loose with her ear-splitting cackle.

I nudged my locker mate. "All she needs is a broom and a good tailwind, if you know what I mean."

Liezel let herself smile.

Once we were safely out of the gym, we stopped in the courtyard to look over our schedules. "What's Lisp?" I asked Liezel. "I have it first period. Is that a speech class?"

"Lisp?" Frowning, she took the card I held out. "Oh, LSP. It stands for 'leadership.' You're in Mr. Tanori's leadership class."

No!

Her Fabulousness and the Royal Court were in that class. Like I said, Big Mess was their kingdom. I did my best to stay out of their way, which is why I had not signed up for leadership class, not even as an alternate.

"How could this have happened?" I blew air out of my cheeks.

"I don't know, but if I were you, I'd be more worried about these next three classes."

I peered over her shoulder. "Why?"

"They're all PE."

Four

I was drawing.

Sitting on our blue sofa, my knees up to support my sketchbook, I began drawing what I remembered most about her: pale green eyes with flecks of gold. There is no sound quite like a newly sharpened pencil on paper. First, the *wissss* of clean lines stroking from the razor sharp point. Then the rapid *woos-woos* of the angle as you fill and shade, lighter in some places, darker in others. Wherever you want, however you want. Where once there was nothing, now there is everything. Emotion, life, beauty, pain, hope—you.

Poof!

Not that there is really anything magical about it. It is work. Every stroke is hard work.

As I sketched, the crisp scent of melting cheddar cheese tickled my nose. On the first day of school we always ate toasted cheese sandwiches with sliced tomatoes for dinner. I couldn't say exactly why or how the tradition started, but I knew when. It was the first day of second grade. The third day of September. Three months to the day after my mother left.

Left.

It makes it sound like she went to the grocery store and will be back any minute. Whenever Aunt Iona says it, her face gets all distorted. She has this way of making "left" sound like "murder." She does it without realizing it. My aunt is a family counselor, so she is very big on expressing your innermost feelings. She thinks if she doesn't constantly remind me that what happened was not my fault, I will be permanently damaged. Aunt Iona can relax. I know nothing was—is—my fault. I know my mother loved—loves—me. It's just she is a restless soul. She can't help it. My mom is a famous travel writer. She gets to fly all over the world and stay in a different hotel every night. It's a glamorous life. How many kids do you know who get Egyptian lotus flower perfume or an aboriginal handmade didgeridoo from Australia for their birthday? Okay, the perfume gave me a rash and the didgeridoo arrived broken, but still . . .

True, it would be nice if my mother stayed in one place for more than a weekend, and it would be even nicer if that place was Oak Harbor, but I am not holding my breath. It's not like I *never* talk to or see my mother. I get a text from her every couple of months, and we talk, maybe, once every six months, depending on where she is and what she's doing. I wish we talked more. I wish when we *did* talk, it was about stuff that mattered, instead of the weather or school. It's hard, wanting to be with a person more than they want to be with you. Especially when that person is your mom. But you can't force somebody to be who you want them to be. The magic only works on you, and even then, there's only so much it can do.

Aunt Iona said in therapeutic terms I was in denial about my mother, so, of course, I giggled and said, "I deny that I'm in denial." I tended to laugh off a lot of my aunt's counseling stuff, particularly the things that are true.

My life is divided into two parts. The one Before Mom and the one After Mom. I was starting to like AM the more I lived it. After Mom was when I first started drawing—faces, mostly. But other things too, like animals and angels. Sketching made me feel like there was a purpose for being. I could sit on the playground at recess and draw and forget, for a while, that nearly every other minute of my life was spent wishing, wishing, wishing my mom would come home. While I drew, I'd steal glances at the other kids on the playground, hoping someone would be brave enough to come over and talk to me. It rarely happened, and when it did, it never led to anything important. Like friendship.

"Who's that?" My dad was hovering over my left shoulder.

"Liezel Sheppard. She's my locker partner."

"Nice eyes. I hope she's better than the girl you had last spring."

He meant Stockholm Ingebrittson, one of Dijon's fringe Somebodies. Stockholm had not appreciated getting assigned a locker mate three-quarters of the way through the school year. Stock also believed anything that was yours was hers—your food, your pens, your books, and especially, your money. It took me a while to figure out I was sharing a locker with a shoplifter, or as I liked to refer to her, Stocklifter.

"A billion times better," I said. "Liezel plays in a rock band."

"A musician, huh?" He headed back into the kitchen. "How are your classes?"

"Uh . . . good. Mrs. Gisborne is making a few minor adjustments."

"How's Waffles?

"Crooked."

He poked his head out of the kitchen. "Everything's okay, though, with your classes?"

"Yeah," I lied, letting the couch cushions consume me. I didn't want to relive the horror. After I'd picked up my schedule from Mrs. Gisborne, my first day of eighth grade had gone from irritating to excruciating.

See, once you notify the counselor's office there's a problem with your schedule, you're supposed to continue going to your assigned classes and wait to be called down to the counseling office. That meant after leadership class (with Adair, thank God!), I was forced to spend the next three hours with Mrs. Notting and Miss Furdy in the gym.

Mrs. Notting coached cheerleading, along with girls' basketball, softball, and volleyball. Miss Furdy was the assistant cheer coach, and handled the track and cross-country teams. They weren't exactly fashionistas. Coach Notting liked to wear nylon, size "small" tracksuits. Too bad *she* was a size large. The pants never hit past her ankles.

Coach Notting chuckled when she saw my schedule card. "I didn't know you liked PE this much, Sherwood."

"They said they'd call me down soon to fix it," I said. "Probably by the end of the day."

Coach Notting clicked her tongue.

"What?"

"Try Thursday."

"Three days? I have to wait *three* days?"

"Maybe a week," added Miss Furdy, shaking her head.

"It can get pretty chaotic trying to sort out all the computer glitches, and yours is a whopper," said the coach. "But don't worry, we'll keep you busy while you're ours."

I didn't like the way she said "while you're ours." Like I was her slave. If I had to clean fungus out of the showers or unravel the Jupiter-sized ball of tangled jump ropes, I was going to drop out of middle school here and now.

"She could be our model," said Miss Furdy.

I definitely did *not* like the sound of that. "I could go to the library," I offered.

"Get suited up, Sherwood," said Coach Notting.

"You'll be our model today as we go over the dress code with each class."

"Uh . . . well . . ."

"You *do* have your PE clothes."

I winced. "It's only the first day of school. I thought—"

"It stated very clearly in your 'Welcome Back to Briar Green' letter that you were to bring your PE clothes on the first day of class so you could place them in your assigned locker."

"There was a letter? I don't remember any—"

Coach Notting sighed. "Excuses, Sherwood, are like belly buttons. Everyone has one and what are they good for?"

"Sorry, I didn't mean—"

"Apologies, Sherwood, are like traffic lights. If there's no change, there can be no progress. Now go get suited up."

"But I didn't—"

"I know, I know. You don't have your clothes." She tossed me a key. "You should be able to find something that fits in the lost-and-found bin in the cabinet behind you."

For the next three hours I had to stand in front of

the PE classes wearing someone else's shirt (ew!) that wouldn't stay down and someone else's shorts (double ew!) that wouldn't stay up. The shirt was so old, it had teeny lint balls stuck to it. The shorts smelled like spoiled milk. Well, I told myself it was spoiled milk. Denial *can* come in handy, now and then. Following each Modeling Session of Torture, the rest of the period was spent playing basketball. I noticed that Coach Notting and Miss Furdy divided the teams by social level: Somebodies and Sortabodies against Nobodies. Naturally, the Nobodies didn't stand a chance. In third period Dijon, Évian, and Venice led their team to a 38 to 8 victory against a very frustrated team of Nobodies. I know, because I was on the Nobodies' team. I scored all eight points. I would have scored more, but my teammate Renata Zickelfoos had coordination issues. She didn't know how to dribble, pass, or shoot. She also had geography issues. Renata couldn't remember which basket was ours. It was a long morning. When it was over, I had come to the conclusion that Coach Notting was like a pimple. Painful, embarrassing, and probably going to leave a scar. But she was right about one thing. I never did get called down to the counseling office.

"Coco Simone?" I heard sizzling. My dad had flipped the toasted cheese. "Dinner's about ready. Set the table?"

"Okay." I laid my drawing pencil on the glass coffee table and flipped to the back cover of my sketchbook. With my thumb I inched a curling scrap of drawing paper from the single pocket. The pencil portrait of her wasn't a very good likeness. The forehead was too big. The eyes too far apart. There was a smudge near her left ear. Still, I *had* done it a long, long time ago, before my mother had left. And it was all I had. I placed the portrait of my mom gently in my palm. Each time I held it, the paper felt a little thinner.

"What a day," I whispered. "Her Fabulousness and the Royal Court are up to their usual tricks. Dijon kicked Fawn out of her own locker. Can you believe that? It looks like she's going to be even more of a pain than last year, if that's possible. And guess what? I've got three periods of PE with Coach Notting. Talk about a nightmare. But don't worry, the counselors will straighten everything out. Dad won't have to call the school or anything. I met my new locker partner. Her name is Liezel. You'd like her. She's nothing like Stocklifter. Oh, and I grew half an inch. Aunt Iona measured me. She says she's pretty sure I grew overnight, but you know how she exaggerates—"

"*Coco?*"

"Coming." Lightly touching my lips to the paper, I slipped my mother back into her pocket and closed the book.

Five

"I'm not doing it, Adair."

"But you promised."

"I did not."

"You said you'd support me when I tried out for cheer."

"I meant from the *bleachers*."

"I don't need you in the bleachers. I need someone to cheer *with* me. Fawn, will you tell her?"

Cheerleading? Was she serious? Ewwww, with three extra *w*'s and a cherry on top. Of all the things in the world I hated, cheerleading was right up there between wolf spiders and flu shots. My first week of school had been horrendous enough without adding cheer to the mix. I'd finally gotten my class schedule sorted out, only to discover I had one class with Fawn (PE), one with Adair (leadership), and three with Her Fabulousness. *Three!* Worse, one of those classes was PE. Worse than worse, I had to get dressed (and undressed!) next to Dijon. She had perfect skin and perfect toes. I had a million arm freckles and crooked toes. The one bright spot in my schedule of despair was learning that Fawn, Adair, and I had the same lunch.

"I can't cheer," I told Adair. "I have absolutely no flexibility. I can't even touch my toes. See?" I threw my chest forward, wriggling my fingers several inches short of my tennis shoes. "I'd ruin it for you, for sure. Fawn, will you tell her?"

Fawn, sitting on the grass with her knees to her chin, pulled her vintage 1970s oatmeal-colored tunic down over her knees. Then she crooked her finger. At me.

Wearily, I went down to her level.

"Last year," Fawn said quietly, "she missed being first alternate by two points."

"So?" A tsunami of a headache was roaring through my brain.

"We're her best friends, and it's our duty to help her fulfill her destiny."

"Not if I don't know any of the cheers."

"You only have to do two for the tryout. Adair can teach them to you right now. It'll be easy."

If it was so easy, how come Fawn wasn't doing it?

I twisted my hoodie strings around my wrists. You didn't have to know Adair long to realize how much she wanted to be a cheerleader. She never wasted a moment standing still if she could be throwing her arms up and twisting and bouncing to a chant only she could hear. It could get annoying, especially in a car. I wanted Adair to pursue her passion. Truly, I did. But why did *her* dream have to involve *my* humiliation?

"Everybody tries out in pairs," said Fawn. "All she needs is someone to stand up and do the cheers with her in front of the judging panel. You don't have to be good at it, Coco. You just have to *do* it."

"Pleeeeease?" said Adair, falling to the ground beside us. "Please be my partner?"

I looked from Adair's hopeful, blue eyes into Fawn's hopeful, brown ones. I had no chance, mainly because there were four big, sad eyes against my two little, weak ones. That, and because I was also sitting on an anthill.

Flicking ants off my ankles, I said, "All right, I'll do it, but I'm wearing my hood up."

"Deal," said Adair.

"And my sunglasses."

"Okay."

"And I refuse to do any cheers that involve barking."

Don't think I didn't catch the "uh-oh" look that passed between them.

Forty-eight minutes later I was in a gym hotter than the orchid house at the arboretum, flapping my arms, kicking my legs, and yelling at the top of my lungs:

> We are the St. Bernards.
> Victory is in the cards.
> Stand tall and raise the roof.
> Paws up! Let's woof, woof, WOOF!

My first thought, as I gazed out into the bleachers filled with about fifty stunned cheerleader wannabes, was someone was going to pay for this. And pay big. Fawn had remained outside, saying she didn't want to make me nervous. Nice try. She knew better than to be anywhere in the vicinity of me when I finished. While Adair and I did our cheers, Her Fabulousness and the Royal Court sat in the front row, pointing and snickering. Even the three judges—Coach Notting, Miss Furdy, and Mrs. Ignazio, an English teacher who coached girls' softball—couldn't hide their grins. I didn't blame them. If there was a cheerleading manual, which there probably was, I could have been the poster girl for every single "don't" in the book. If I wasn't hopping on the wrong foot or saying the wrong words, then I was facing the wrong direction. Only one thing kept me from bolting from the gym as fast as my uncoordinated feet could take me: Adair. She was smiling bigger than I had ever seen her smile. Her movements were graceful and perfectly synchronized with her words. She oozed school spirit. Even her competition couldn't help but love her. The other girls were cheering along with her. Fawn was right. *This* was where Adair belonged. It was her destiny. So, for her, I stayed. And barked. And made a complete goober out of myself, bopping around and shouting:

> S-T B-E-R.
> I say, S-T B-E-R.
> Yeah, yeah, yeah.
> S-T B-E-R.
> I say, N-A-R-D-S.
> Go, go, go!
> Goooooo, Briar Green!
> 'Cause we the machine
> That's gonna steamroll over you!

Who wrote this stuff?

Adair finished our second cheer with a back handspring and a full split! I finished our second cheer with a gazelle leap, and split the rear of my jeans.

When a bunch of girls began applauding for Adair, Her Fabulousness and her court turned around and gave them nasty glares. The girls dropped their hands and looked anywhere but at us. I struggled out of my hoodie and tied the sleeves around my waist to hide my unfortunate accident.

"Thank you, ladies," said Coach Notting, briskly marking on her score sheet with a pencil.

Adair clung to me as we walked away. "How do you think it went?"

With just three pairs of girls left to audition, I could honestly say, "You're going to look amazing in green and silver."

My friend beamed.

"Cadence and Willow were great too," I said. Cadence Steele and Willow Christopher were two Nobodies who had tried out ahead of us. Willow had tons of energy and could jump higher than my waist! And Cadence had the best dance moves of anyone out there, except Adair. "I bet they'll make it with you."

"Don't be so sure," muttered Adair.

I understood. The competition was tough, and the Somebodies had the edge. Still, most of the Somebodies had been less than stellar. Her Fabulousness didn't make any mistakes in front of the judges, but she was, clearly, bored. Dijon hadn't put an ounce of enthusiasm into her cheers. She didn't yell. She spoke. Once, she even yawned in the middle of a cheer. Évian had plenty of spirit, all right, but was worse than me when it came to remembering the words. Venice and Truffle couldn't stop giggling throughout their entire audition. They didn't even finish their second cheer. If ever there was a chance for one or two or maybe even three talented Nobodies to make the team, this was the year!

"When will you know the results?" I asked Adair.

"Let's see . . . probably next Monday or Tuesday. Mrs. Rivkin usually posts the list on the ASB bulletin board outside the cafeteria." She glanced up at the clock. "I've got to get going. My mom will be waiting. Thanks for cheering with me, Coco. I couldn't have done it without you."

"Anytime." I crossed my eyes. "Kidding!"

Fawn was in the same spot on the grass where we'd

left her. Seeing me approach, she lowered her e-reader. "How'd it go?"

"Adair was brilliant."

"And you?"

"Could be the first girl in Big Mess cheerleading history to get a negative score."

She tilted her head. "Why are you walking funny?"

"To keep *this* from getting worse." I whipped around and flipped up the back of my jacket.

"Oh ho, ho!"

"You should know I'm plotting my revenge against you."

"Thanks for the warning," she said, reaching for her backpack. "You plot. I'll sew." Fawn was going to be a famous fashion designer one day. She was always attaching all kinds of lace, fringe, beads, and assorted dangly things to her vintage outfits, which meant she carried a needle and thread with her for when the lace, fringe, beads, and assorted dangly things fell off.

We had about forty minutes before Fawn's mom was due to pick us up. Fawn said that was plenty of time to fix my seam, so we went into the girls' locker room. I led us to my PE locker in the last row, sat down on the bench, and took off my jeans. Fawn got to work on the repair. It was chilly sitting in my underwear. I was debating whether I should put on my gym shorts when we heard a clang.

"It must have been ninety degrees in that gym."

I knew that voice. It was Miss Furdy.

"My head is pounding."

And Mrs. Ignazio.

"I think I may have some aspirin in my purse."

And Coach Notting.

"The cheer judges," I hissed at Fawn. "They're here!"

Her head shot up, a piece of thread hanging from her mouth.

We weren't doing anything wrong, but it sure felt that way. We could hear Coach Notting unlocking the door to the office. "That's one of the biggest turnouts we've ever had for cheer."

"It's going to be tough narrowing down the field," said Mrs. Ignazio. "Some of the girls were wonderful dancers, and others had more athletic ability. And then there were those who lit up the room with their energy, like the Christopher girl. Now, she's what cheerleading is all about."

Mrs. Ignazio liked Willow. Our Willow. Nobody Willow!

"Yes," said Miss Furdy, dragging out the word so I knew a "but" was coming. "A sparkling personality is great, but we must take other things into consideration too."

"Other things?" Mrs. Ignazio seemed confused.

"You know, like . . . well, I hate to say it, but we do have to look at physical appearance as well."

My breath caught in my throat.

Unbelievable!

Fawn's mouth had formed a big O, no doubt, to match mine. We were both thinking the same thing. We knew what Miss Furdy meant, and she was wrong. Willow was not fat. She had muscular thighs, sure, but that's because she swam and played on the girls' soccer team. And even if she wasn't a size two, so what? In fact, *not* being perfect would make her a good role model for the younger girls. The important thing was, Willow would be an outstanding cheerleader. I wanted to leap to my feet, march into the coach's office, and tell them exactly that. But I didn't. For one thing, I was in my underwear. For another, it could get Adair disqualified. If the judges saw me, they'd think I had deliberately eavesdropped. We had to get out of there without being seen. But how? Coach Notting's office

48

was between us and the only exit that wasn't a fire door.

My heart started flailing.

My palms felt sticky.

My legs were starting to turn a weird shade of blotchy violet.

I wasn't sure what to do. Fawn and I were trapped in the Big Mess girls' locker room with no way out!

Six

I mouthed the word "hurry" to Fawn. Not that she needed *me* to tell her. The sewing needle was flying through denim.

"What did you think of the Steele girl?" asked Coach Notting.

"Steele? Steele. Steele." Miss Furdy was searching. "Cadence Steele. Here she is. Let's see . . . I wrote down 'good dancer,' but for some reason I can't seem to recall her. She wasn't the one wearing sunglasses, was she?"

"No," Coach Notting cut in. "That was Coco Sherwood."

Wincing, I cocked my head.

"Ah, right, the girl with the coordination issues," said Miss Furdy. "It didn't look like she'd put in much practice time, but I liked her effort level. She didn't give up, even after she made mistakes."

Me? Give up? Never.

Well, if it hadn't been for Adair . . .

Miss Furdy read my mind. "Of course, it helped that she was cheering with the Clarke girl."

"Adair *was* impressive," said Coach Notting.

Fawn's hand paused in midair. She looked at me and smiled.

I pumped my fist. *Yes!*

"She certainly was," said Miss Furdy. "Very bubbly and vivacious."

Yes and more yes!

"She's quite striking," said Mrs. Ignazio. "And her dancing and gymnastic skills were excellent."

YES!

I jumped off the bench and thrust my arms skyward. There could be no doubt now that Adair was going to make the squad. Finally, a Nobody was going to live her dream, and I had helped to make it come true! Pride surged through every limb in my body.

"There's no denying Adair Clarke *was* good," said Coach Notting with a long sigh. "But . . ."

I froze.

"It's too bad she isn't, you know . . ."

No, I didn't know.

"What?" asked Mrs. Ignazio.

Yes, what? WHAT?

"One of our more popular girls."

"Oh!"

That was Fawn. Not that I blamed her. My friend slapped a hand over her mouth. I lunged for my jeans. We had to get out of there. *Now.*

"I thought we were supposed to fill out our judging sheets without discussion so we wouldn't influence one another," said Mrs. Ignazio, her voice tight.

"Yes, of course," said Coach Notting. "We must keep everything fair."

Fair? Buttoning my jeans, I had to stifle my own cry. *Fair?* It was pretty obvious what was going on here. Her Fabulousness and the Royal Court, along with six other Somebodies, would get all ten spots on cheer staff. Why? Because that's how things worked in our world. Status was more important than skill. Image was more important than heart. There was nothing "fair" about this process.

Not. One. Thing.

I signaled for Fawn to follow me. We took the long way around the last row of lockers, creeping along the outside wall until we reached Coach Notting's office. Hunched next to the open door, I could see the reflec-

52

tion in the picture window. Three heads were bent. Coach Notting was the only one facing our way. I slowly let all the air out of my body, then quickly tiptoed past the doorframe. I didn't breathe again until I was safely on the other side. Peering through the glass, I saw Miss Furdy had turned and lifted her head. She was squinting at the door. I put up my hand to tell Fawn to stay still.

Thankfully, Fawn was watching the glass too.

After a few seconds Miss Furdy went back to work. I gave Fawn the okay sign. Instead of lightly stepping, as I had done, Fawn decided to take one big leap. It might have worked, too, if the strap of her backpack hadn't whacked the door.

"Hey!" called Coach Notting.

Fawn skidded to a stop.

"What are you doing here?" asked Miss Furdy.

"Me? I . . . uh . . ."

"She must be our runner," said Coach Notting.

Fawn gulped hard. "Huh?"

"Did Mrs. Rivkin send you?"

Coach Furdy assumed Fawn was Mrs. Rivkin's teaching assistant, here to pick up the judging sheets to take to the main office.

"Um . . ." Her mouth gaping, Fawn turned to me.

I bobbed my head.

So Fawn bobbed *her* head.

"Hold on one moment. We're almost done."

Hearing footsteps, I backed into the shadows.

"Here you go," said Coach Notting. "Guard it with your life."

"O-okay." Fawn took the envelope and raced out of the locker room. I was a millisecond behind her.

"Oh my God, oh my God, oh my God," Fawn screeched. She was clutching a big, gold envelope to her chest. "We'd better drop this off before we get in trouble." She steamed across the courtyard.

"Fawn?" I tore after her. "Fawn, wait—"

"Coco, be careful. We were in such a rush, I dropped the needle. It might still be in your jeans somewhere—"

"You know what you've got there, don't you?"

"Of course."

"Well?"

"Well, what?"

"Don't you want to know?"

"We can't. It's against the rules. Here comes Ava, anyway."

Ava Tibbs was Mrs. Rivkin's sixth-period teaching assistant.

"We've got the judging sheets for cheer tryouts," Fawn called to her, waving the envelope.

"Could you do me a big fave and run them down to Mrs. Rivkin?" huffed Ava. "I'm already late for tennis practice."

"We're on it," I said, snatching the envelope from Fawn.

Now it was her turn to catch up to me. I yanked open the door to C wing.

"Where are you going? The office is the other way."

"Just taking a little detour." I punched the door to the girls' bathroom and went inside.

"Geez, Coco, can't you wait to go until *after* we've dropped off the judging sheets?"

I went down the row of stalls, carefully checking under each door. When I was certain we were alone, I popped up the two pronged clips on the back of the envelope and lifted the flap.

That's when Fawn clued in as to why we were really here. "Coco, no!"

"I only want to see the final scores."

"If someone finds out, we could get in big trouble."

"You're not going to tell, are you?"

"No, but—"

"Neither am I, so no one is going to find out. Besides, it's destiny. You said so yourself."

"I said *what*?"

"You said it was our duty as friends to help Adair fulfill her destiny. Well, whatever that destiny is, it's inside this envelope. So couldn't we be of more help to her if we knew what fate had in store?"

Fawn tucked her magenta stripe behind one ear, then immediately yanked it out again. "I'm not sure."

I reached into the envelope. "If you don't want to know, don't look."

Fawn spun away. "This is wrong. This is *so* wrong."

There was a note on top from Coach Notting to Mrs. Rivkin. In it, the coach directed the secretary to place the individual judging sheets in a confidential file and the final tally sheet in Coach Notting's box. I flipped past the judges' individual scoring sheets to find the final tally sheet at the bottom of the stack. Except for the date, it was blank.

"Uh-oh."

Fawn spun back. "What is it?"

"The final scores aren't here."

"I could have told you that. See, all of the judges score each girl independently, then Mrs. Rivkin adds everything up. That way, none of the judges knows how any of the other judges scored the contestants. It's supposed to keep everything fair."

There was that word again. Everybody kept saying it, but it didn't seem to count for much.

I took out my cell phone and turned it on.

"What are you doing?"

"Scrolling to my calculator. I want to see how Adair did."

"You can't do that!"

"Why not?"

"Because . . . because . . . you just can't. Only Mrs. Rivkin can add up the scores. Those are the rules." She lunged for the phone, but I was a hair quicker.

"You're going to get us in trouble," Fawn whined. "Coach Notting will find out, and we'll be stuck with Mrs. Pescatori in the detention room knitting dog hats for the rest of the semester. We might even be suspended or"—she gasped—"expelled!"

"I'm just doing a little arithmetic," I said, sliding down the wall so I could sit on the floor. "They don't expel you for doing math."

Fawn started pacing. "I've never been expelled before. Does that affect your grade point average?"

"Shhh."

"If we're expelled, we'll have to go to Olympic View. I don't want to be a honeybee. I'm allergic to bees—"

"Yow!"

"What?"

I rubbed my rear. "I just found your needle."

Fawn collapsed on the floor beside me. "Come on, Coco. Did she make it or not?"

I *knew* she wanted to know!

"Hold on." I needed a pen and paper. After several minutes of scribbling in the back of my math notebook, I glanced up into worried, brown eyes. "I don't think so."

"How could she not make it? You said she was brilliant!"

"She *was*. But see here? Dijon, Venice, Truffle, Évian, Dover, uh . . . Lisbon, Monaco, Stocklifter, let's see— oh, and Geneva and Perrier—all got an average score of ninety or above."

Fawn's lips disappeared. "You mean, all the Some-bodies."

"Yep."

"What did Adair get?"

"Um . . . eighty-eight."

"Not again." Fawn laid her head against the wall. "Two points."

"I was adding pretty fast. I could have made a mistake. . . ."

"She's wanted this for so long. It's all she's talked about since the third grade. To wait another year is going to crush her. And then she's going to have to compete with even more girls in high school . . ."

"I'll add again." I cleared the calculator.

"This is going to crush her," Fawn said again. "It's not fair. She's better than all the Somebodies put together. If anybody deserves to be a Big Mess cheerleader, it's Adair."

I didn't know where the idea came from. One moment it wasn't there and then—*zing*—it was.

My fingers on the keypad, I slowly lifted my head. "She still can be."

Fawn probed my eyes, and I knew what she was thinking. Sneaking a peek at the judges' score sheets in the girls' C-wing bathroom was one thing. What I was proposing was on a whole new level.

Fawn swallowed hard. "You mean, cheat?"

I knew what cheating was. It was copying someone else's homework when you'd forgotten yours. It was begging kids who'd already taken a test you were about to take, "What were the questions?" It was cutting passages from an Internet site and pasting them into your homework. That was cheating. And I didn't do it. Not ever. But this was different.

"The judges are the ones who are cheating, Fawn. You said so yourself. Adair has earned this. Nobody deserves it more than she does."

Fawn began tying the fringe of her tunic into knots. "I know, but—"

"We'd be righting a wrong. We'd be battling social discrimination. We'd be taking a stand for all the Nobodies who can't fight for themselves."

It was a good speech.

I waited for Fawn to list a hundred reasons why I'd never get away with it—all of them ending in, "You'll get in trouble, Coco." But Fawn didn't lecture me. She didn't try to scare me with her endless list of possible punishments. Instead, my best friend tucked her magenta-dyed stripe behind her ear, and said softly, very softly, "Okay." It might have been more believable if her chin hadn't been quivering when she'd said it.

No matter. She'd said it.

I knew then, destiny wasn't something mysterious

or strange or spiritual. It wasn't someplace far away or meant for someone else. Destiny was here, in my hands, for me to guide.

All I needed was a drop of courage and a good eraser.

Fortunately, I had both.

Seven

"The name of this class is what?" Mr. Tanori scanned the room.

We all looked at one another. Was he joking? A trick question? Maybe Mr. Tanori had bumped his head on the lights. He was ridiculously tall.

"Leadership?" ventured Breck.

"Exactly. So what qualities do you think a good leader should have? How about you, Renata?"

"Um . . ." Sitting in the last seat in the row to the right of mine, Renata Zickelfoos stopped playing her invisible piano. She began to swing the long ends of her sweater sleeves. Renata always wore several layers of sweaters, topped off with a long blue scarf wrapped several times around her neck. She didn't bother to take her hair out of the scarf, so it created a bulge just below her ears. It reminded me of a flying saucer— a flying saucer made of limp, reddish-brown hair.

Renata wriggled her nose to slide a pair of red rectangular plastic glasses back up into place. "I gueth a leader thould be willing to lithen." Whenever she had to speak in public, Renata had difficulty with her *s*'s. But we knew what she meant.

"Exactly." Mr. Tanori wrote "good listener" on the whiteboard.

Venice, to my right, jabbed Dijon, who was in front of her. "Did you hear what Renata Piñata said? Lithening is important."

Giggling, Dijon straightened her silver tiara with the fake diamonds. It was Friday, after all. "Did you thay thomething, Venith? I wathn't lithening."

Renata's cheeks turned the color of a flamingo, which, by the way, was Dijon's makeup color of the week.

Yes, Dijon had put up her beauty board. And yes, I had sworn a sacred oath to never again lay eyes on it, but it was an impossible promise to keep. It's like when you see a crash on the freeway. Your first impulse is to turn away so you won't see anything horrible, but then something, some little morbid part of you, *has* to take a quick peek and—auggh! Splashes of blood and broken glass and twisted metal. And regret. So much regret. Same thing with Dijon's locker. Each time I went by it,

I told myself, "I won't look, I won't look, I won't look," and then I'd walk by and—bam!—my eyes automatically swerved to that dumb heart-shaped whiteboard:

Hey, Peeps!
Buy FlowerPower
blush #9, Flamingo Pink
XXOO,
Dijon

Ew.

I hated myself for looking. But, at least, *I* had some dignity. It was a sure bet that by Monday, most of the girls at Big Mess would be wearing FlowerPower blush #9, Flamingo Pink.

Double ew.

"What else makes a strong leader?" asked Mr. Tanori.

"Respect," I said loudly, staring straight ahead.

"Good, Coco."

To my left, Adair called out, "Honesty."

A lump rose in my throat. Suddenly I couldn't breathe. I started choking. Adair reached across the aisle to pat me on the back. As I coughed, I could hear kids calling out more suggestions.

"A leader is organized."

"Considerate of others."

"Has clear goals."

I pounded my own chest. *Breathe! Breathe!*

"Inspires people."

"Shares responsibility."

"Isn't afraid of criticism."

"Great," said Mr. Tanori, racing to write down everyone's ideas. "Keep them coming."

"You okay, Sherwood?"

Through watery eyes, I saw the freckled nose of Breck Hanover. He was crouched next to me. Eyelashes flicked behind sandy bangs. He smelled like peanuts.

"I think so," I croaked, though my fingers were all tingly and my head felt like an overinflated balloon.

"Need some water?"

I took a few ragged breaths. "I'm all right," I said hoarsely.

"Easy, Sherwood," he said, patting my shoulder twice before going back to his desk.

Adair's voice tickled my ear. "He is so crushing on you."

"Is not." I gagged. "He likes Venice."

"Wrong-o, Coco. Venice likes Breck. *Huge* difference. I know a crush when I spy one, and this is a classic crushing."

"Right."

"Would you like proof?"

"Always."

"Exhibit A: Remember how he threw candy at us at orientation? That's the number one thing boys do when they like you."

"They chuck Whoppers?"

"Not just Whoppers. Jelly beans, spit wads, erasers—you name it. Boys are throwers, by nature."

"I thought they were burpers, by nature."

She crossed her eyes, but didn't disagree. "Exhibit B: He rushed to your side when you had a coughing fit, but had to pretend he wasn't too interested, in case you didn't like him, so what did he do?"

I shook my head. She was warping through the galaxy all by herself here.

"He called you by your last name. That's the second thing boys do when they like you. There's a whole article about it in the fall issue of *Modern Teen*. I'll loan you my copy if you want—"

"Ladies?" Mr. Tanori was pointing his pen at us.

"Sorry," Adair and I said at the same time.

"Anyway," said our teacher, "I know the general impression is that this class is all about making signs for pep rallies and assemblies. But it's not. It's much more. In here, you'll be learning skills you can put to use in whatever leadership roles you take on in life. Why is being a leader important? Because strong leadership skills allow you to take an active part in making a difference in the world." Mr. Tanori looked at me. "There's an old proverb that goes: 'One who walks in another's tracks leaves no footprints.' I want all of you to learn to make your own footprints."

I liked the sound of that. I wasn't exactly sure what I was supposed to do with it, but I liked it.

Mr. Tanori continued. "This year, we will be taking a bigger role in making some school improvements, thanks to the generosity of our PTA. . . ."

Was Adair right? Did Breck really have a crush on me?

And if he did, did I want him to have a crush on me?

I'd have to think about it. Boys seemed like *way* more hassle than they were worth. The ones I knew were always kickboxing in the hallway or opening their mouths while they were eating to show you their half-chewed food. Most looked like they wore their clothes to bed and smelled like they hadn't showered in days. There were some nice ones too, of course, like Nobodies Curtis Desidario and Alan Dwyer, but finding them was like finding the toy in the cereal box. You had to dig deep. Really deep.

Dijon had a boyfriend. Naturally. His name was C. K. Stenmont. He was a star soccer player. They held hands as he walked her to her classes. I couldn't imagine letting a boy wrap his fingers around mine. Have you noticed boys' fingernails? Crustomatic to the max. I've never in my life seen a boy wash his hands. In Parker's case, he probably couldn't figure out how to work the tap.

If, by chance, Breck did like me and if, by chance, I did like that he liked me, there was one obstacle to our possible mutual likeness. He was a Somebody. I was a Nobody. Somebodies and Nobodies weren't allowed to be friends, let alone be boyfriend/girlfriend. It was against the code. It would never work.

"Coco, can I be in your group?" asked Renata, flopping her big sleeves at me. Her seaweed bangs hung between her eyes and her red glasses.

I didn't really want to say yes, but I didn't want to be rude, either. "Uh, yeah . . . sure," I said, following Adair's lead and turning my desk around.

Renata moved her desk to connect with ours. The

moment Renata plopped down, she began to play her invisible piano. It was going to be a long period.

"Now, remember," said Mr. Tanori. "Brainstorming means everyone's ideas are valid. Write down everything your group members say. No judgments at this stage, okay?"

Adair looked at me. "Do you want to write or should I?"

"I will. Uh . . . what are we brainstorming?"

She snickered. "Weren't paying attention, huh? I guess you had other stuff on your mind. Or should I say other people."

"Just tell me."

"The PTA is going to pay for a school improvement project, so we're supposed to come up with a bunch of ideas, like new turf for the soccer field or new boards for chess club—stuff like that. The class is going to vote, pick our favorite, and present it to the PTA."

"I think we should paint a mural over that awful orange wall in the cafeteria," said Renata. She glanced up, but her fingers never stopped moving. It was starting to get on my nerves.

"Good idea," said Adair. "Coco, you could design it." She turned to Renata. "She's a really talented artist. She's especially good with faces."

"Nah," I said shyly, writing the idea in my notebook.

"That would be so incredible," said Adair, bouncing. "Imagine a huge wall of different faces blending together. . . ."

"One second," said Renata. "Aren't you forgetting something? We have to get the class to agree—the *whole* class." She tipped her head toward Dijon's group. "I've got a better chance of getting elected fall queen."

Renata was right, of course. Social rules dictated that any time a class vote was called for, everyone was required to vote for the most popular Somebody in the room. Dijon's idea, whatever it was, would win.

Breck popped up from behind Adair. He glanced at me over my friend's shoulder. "Can I be in your group?"

"Sure," said Adair with a wink to me.

"Breck!" Dijon snapped her fingers. "You're with us."

"Sorry. Next time," said Breck, flicking his bangs out of his eyes.

Whatever. I lifted a shoulder. And turned away.

They were gray.

Anyway, like I said. Too much hassle. Would never work.

I meant his eyes. They were gray.

Eight

"What kind of soup do they have?"

I set my tray on the table beside Adair and across from Fawn. "Can't you tell by the beans?"

"Chicken," Fawn and Adair said together, then laughed.

Adair peered into my bowl. "It looks like antifreeze."

"And smells like wet dog," said Fawn.

"It was either this or the mystery-meat chimichanga."

My friends nodded to confirm I'd made the right choice. I crumbled four packages of crackers into my soup to soak up the sludge.

Through a thin curtain of rising steam I grinned at Fawn. From across the table she grinned back. It was strange, sharing a secret with her. Adair, Fawn, and I had never hidden anything from one another before. Unless, of course, the two of them had a secret I didn't know about, which they probably did because they had known each other since the fifth grade.

Truth was, I smiled to hide my fear. I had done something else—something not even Fawn knew about. And though I didn't want to admit it, I had begun to regret it almost from the moment Fawn left the girls' bathroom to deliver the envelope to Mrs. Rivkin. What if, in my rush to finish, I'd made an error? What if Mrs. Rivkin didn't follow my instructions? What if she suspected something was up? What if Coach Notting, Miss Furdy, or Mrs. Ignazio had gone to the office after we'd left?

Since yesterday afternoon, a million "what ifs" had been puncturing my brain. And it was beginning to hurt. Fawn was the only link between the judges and Mrs. Rivkin. If any one of my "what ifs" came true, the trail would lead the administration straight to us. Fawn's guilty heart would spill her guts in record time. Knowing how well organized she was, she probably already had her confession written and had made individual copies for Dr. Adams, Mr. Falkner, and Mrs. Pescatori in detention. We were never going to get away with this. *Never.*

The temperature under my hoodie was starting to rise.

"I can't sit still," said Adair, jiggling. "I wish they would post the cheer results. This is killing me."

"Me too," I murmured, fanning myself with my napkin.

"Monday is three whole days away."

I wished Adair would stop bobbing. She was shaking the whole table. I was getting seasick. Across from me Fawn was sipping her chocolate milk and going up and down. Up and down.

I struggled to escape my stifling hoodie. "Hey, Liezel's in the lunch line."

"Say that three times fast," teased Fawn.

Adair gave it a try. "Liezel's in the lunch line. Liezel's in the lunch line. Liezel's in the lee line—aaugggh!"

I didn't know she had first lunch. "Let's ask her to eat with us," I said.

Fawn let out a ghostlike sigh.

Adair was more direct. "Do we have to?"

I looked from one to the other. "You don't like her?"

"It's not that we don't like her." Fawn sucked in her lower lip. "It's that she's sort of . . ."

"Beige," said Adair.

Color code for boring.

"With blue stripes," said Fawn. "She's always got on a sad face."

"Add some purple stripes," said Adair. "She's accident-prone. Every time I pass her in the hallway, she's picking her stuff up off the floor."

Fawn peeled the lid off her vanilla pudding. "You know what happens when you mix beige, purple, and blue. You get—"

"Brown," I finished.

Brown was worse than beige. Brown was death.

Was it a coincidence that brown-haired Liezel was wearing a dark-brown sweater with brown pants and brown boots? Even her backpack was brown. Adair and Fawn bowed their heads at the tragedy.

"Wait a minute," I said, coming to my senses. "She might wear brown, but she *isn't* brown. You want proof?"

"Always," said Adair.

"Exhibit A: She's not accident-prone. Venice tripped her in front of everybody in the gym, and now she's got the Royal Court doing it too—every chance they get. They think it's funny."

"No!" Fawn exhaled in horror.

"That's just mean." Adair dumped out her veggie chips onto a napkin.

"Exhibit B: She plays guitar in a rock band. A *high-school* rock band."

Fawn's spoon halted in midair. Adair looked up from sorting her veggie chips. She liked to arrange them in little piles according to color: orange (carrot chips), green (spinach chips), and yellow (potato chips).

"She does?"

"Seriously?"

As Liezel carried her tray to the cashier, Adair's eyes tracked her with new admiration. "She never said anything to anybody," she said, surprised.

I opened another package of crackers. "Actually, she's had a poster tacked up to our locker all week," I replied.

"Liezel!" Adair waved. "Come sit with us."

Fawn scooted her stuff down to make room.

"Hi," said Liezel, sliding onto the bench. "Thanks for the 911. I just got switched to this lunch and thought for sure I was going to get stuck in the boonies with Mr. Quigley. Did you hear? He's got an MP3 player now. It can hold, like, five thousand pictures of Clawed Monet."

We groaned.

"Liezel, do you really play in a rock band?" asked Adair.

"Uh-huh. I play guitar. I sing and write songs, too." She glanced at me. I knew she wanted me to say something about her music, but I couldn't. I hadn't yet listened to her CD. I had meant to, even took it out of the jewel case, but I was too afraid to play it. What if the band was terrible?

Fawn's mouth was open. "You mean, you play in public?"

"Of course. That's the whole point, Fawn. We just played at my church's Labor Day picnic." Her grin faded. "We sent in an audition CD to play at the Big Mess fall dance, but we never heard back. I guess the committee chose another band."

"Yeeeeooooooooooow!"

I was pretty sure the shout had come from the other side of the cafeteria, near the door. Or maybe from the hallway outside.

"It's probably Parker and Todd wrestling again," said Adair.

"Or skateboarding inside again," offered Fawn.

"Or sword fighting with Todd's drumsticks again," said Liezel.

We could go on all day. With those two spit wads the possibilities were endless.

A few seconds later there was another scream. This one had a slightly higher pitch and much more energy behind it.

"Eeeeeeeek!"

That had definitely come from the hallway. This time, Her Fabulousness and the Royal Court quickly packed up and headed out the door—but not too quickly. It wasn't good form for a Somebody to appear too eager to go anywhere.

I looked for Mr. Quigley, our lunchroom monitor. He was on the far side of the cafeteria showing his cat photos to a couple of captive sixth graders. He didn't seem concerned about the shrieks coming from the hall.

"Auuuggggh!"

"What is going on out there?" squealed Adair at the exact moment Évian went by, hurrying to catch up to Dijon.

Évian turned our way and said dryly, "Cheer results."

A hard jolt went through my body. It felt like lightning, but it was probably Adair, yanking off my right arm. "They posted early!"

Color draining from her face, Fawn was frozen to her seat. I had to clap my hands in front of her face to bring her back to reality. "Come on, Fawn, we're going with Adair to check the cheer results."

"O-okay."

I wished she would stop looking so guilty. We had nothing to feel guilty about. Right?

As the four of us made our way across the cafeteria, Adair, who was still firmly glued to my arm, kept repeating, "I can't look, I can't look, I can't look."

"If you don't look, you'll never know," said Liezel.

"Okay, I'll look."

She would, however, have to wait. A traffic jam, several girls deep, blocked the ASB bulletin board. Some of the girls were scanning for their names. Some were scanning for the name of someone they knew. Most, eventually, dropped their arms or heads and silently fell away. When the last of the bodies moved aside, I put my fingers on Adair's spine and pushed her forward.

Fawn, Liezel, and I huddled together. I tried to stay calm, but the beans from my soup kept doing tumbling passes in my stomach. Also, the loop of "what ifs" had started in again from the beginning. What if, in my rush to finish, I'd made an error? What if Mrs. Rivkin didn't follow my instructions? What if she suspected something was up? What if Coach Notting, Miss Furdy, or Mrs. Ignazio had gone to the office after we'd left?

I wasn't going to get away with this, was I?

Nobodies never got away with anything, especially when it involved pulling one over on the Somebodies. Something like what I had done had probably never before been attempted in middle-school history. I wiped my sweaty palms on the front of my jeans. What had I been thinking? No way, no how was this ever going to work.

Adair was charging at us. "I made it!" She leaped into our arms. Her voice was muffled in my shoulder. "You were there with me every step of the way, Coco."

She had *no* idea.

I smiled at Fawn, not to hide my worries but for real. Wiping her forehead with an exaggerated motion, she smiled back.

We had actually *done* it! A couple of Nobodies had changed the course of Big Mess history. Adair was so excited, she couldn't stop squealing and hopping and hugging. I, however, was completely exhausted. Manipulating the world takes a lot out of a person.

"I don't believe it." Willow Christopher turned from the bulletin board. She looked at us, her expressionless face a chalky pink. "I never thought . . . My mom said I shouldn't try out. She said I'd get my heart broken. My sister said I wasn't the right size. . . . I mean, you hope but never in a million, trillion years do you think it's possible and then . . . and then . . ."

"You make it," I whispered.

A tear rolled down her left cheek. "You make it." Trembling hands came to her mouth. "Oh my God, Coco, I made it. I MADE IT!" Willow threw her arms around me and squeezed and squeezed and squeezed until I was certain three or four vital organs were going to burst. She released me so quickly, I stumbled backward into Liezel. "Has anyone told Cadence?" asked Willow. "She's going to flip when she finds out—seriously flip!"

"Cadence? Uh . . . you mean, Cadence is on the squad too?" Fawn moved in to read the post for herself. Her head swiveled to me. "Cadence and Willow *both* made cheer. How about that, Coco?"

"How about that?" I said meekly. Now she knew my secret. I had changed a few more scores than we had agreed on. I couldn't help myself.

Arms outstretched, Willow sailed away. She moved seamlessly through clusters of kids standing in the hall, twirling once to the right, then once to the left, before continuing on her way. It was anything but a middle-school dance. It was the kind of dance you did when you were six years old, and you didn't notice or care if people were watching.

Liezel sighed. "That's a girl in the clouds."

From now on, I knew Willow's life was going to be different. Not because she was a cheerleader—well, partly because she was a cheerleader, but mostly because she was free. She wasn't a Nobody anymore. She was just Willow. Purely Willow.

And I, Coco Simone Sherwood, had helped her to claim that independence.

I felt warm. Electric. Alive.

Willow was at the end of the hall, turning the corner. Still dancing. Still floating above us. Five fluttering fingertips were the last of her to disappear.

Nine

After opening our mailbox, I pulled out a couple of bills and a pile of junk mail. A yellow slip of paper fell to the ground.

Ooooh, a package!

I stuck my mailbox key into another large box at the bottom of the row, swung the door wide, and took out a short, square box. The package was addressed to me. I recognized the handwriting: It was my mother's. I took the box inside our apartment and set it on the end of the granite countertop. The upper right-hand corner was stamped with the word "Kyoto." There was no return address.

My mom always sent me cool stuff from wherever she was, and usually I tore right into it. So why not today? What was I waiting for?

I wasn't sure.

I went to my room. Dash was sleeping—a caramel-colored fluff ball barely visible under his burrow of shavings. After I filled his feeder with hamster pellets and gave him fresh water, he stirred a bit, then went back to sleep.

Restless, I went back out into the kitchen. Yep. The box was still there.

Taking my sketchbook out of my backpack, I headed outside to sit on our balcony. I had nothing against balconies, though I longed for a front porch. We had one. Once. Before Mom. It had a white, wooden love swing that hung from the rafters by two chains. I used to spend my summers on that porch, playing tea party with my dolls and watching people stroll past with their dogs. "Don't go off the porch, Coco," my mom would call out the kitchen window if I ventured too close to the steps. It was hard to obey her, especially when a golden Lab puppy stopped to sniff our bushes or I heard the ice-cream truck blaring "The Farmer in the Dell" slightly off-key. I knew, even then, there was so much waiting for me beyond those stairs. I guess that's why I missed them. A front porch lets you open your arms to what's coming toward you. A balcony is only good for watching what is going away.

I took a seat on one of the green plastic chairs on our third-floor balcony. In no hurry, I began to sketch an extreme close-up of the black-and-white bark that papered the birch trees next to the railing.

All afternoon I hadn't been able to stop thinking about Willow and Adair. I had known they were going to be thrilled to make cheer, of course, but I'd never dreamed they'd be so completely . . . What was the word I was looking for?

"Ecstatic"? "Radiant"? "Transformed"?

Transformed.

That was it. In an instant, it seemed, everything about them had changed, from their faces to their attitudes to their movements. And all it had taken was a single victory. Just one. As I began drawing a garden spider weaving her web in the eaves, I wondered, wouldn't it be something if every Nobody at Big Mess could feel the way Adair and Willow felt? Even for a little while? Even for a minute? It would be more than something. It would be everything.

I let my hand draw whatever it wanted. I did not stop it, even when I knew what it was up to. Those were my rules of art. Never interfere. After about an hour my page was filled with several images—the rippling black-

and-white birch bark, a mottled brown spider hanging from fragile threads, and a pinched face hidden behind rectangular glasses and flying saucer hair.

Renata.

I laughed out loud. If anyone needed transformation, it was Renata. But helping that particular Nobody was going to take a lot more than a calculator and an eraser. I wasn't sure I was ready for a challenge like Renata. Not now. Maybe not ever.

I looked at my watch. My dad was late.

Closing my sketchbook, I went inside and stared at the package for a few more minutes.

For goodness' sake, it's not going to bite or blow up. Just open it.

I got a paring knife and cut into the thick tape on the seam, pulling apart the top flaps. Digging through a layer of bubble wrap, I took out a white shirt box and slipped off the top. There was a note.

Dear Coco,
I hope you like the kimono. Don't you just love
the color? The little silk pouch isn't a purse. It's
a charm. The Japanese call them "omamori."
In Japan, parents and grandparents often

*give their children omamori on the first day of
school to bring good luck or protection. They
may tuck a piece of paper with prayers or good
wishes inside the bag, but NO PEEKING!
You are not supposed to open the pouch, or
the luck will disappear. Kids attach omamori
to their cell phones or backpacks. I see them
everywhere here! So here's a little luck to get
your new school year off to a great start. Hope
it's going well. I'm off to my next assignment in
Taiwan and will call soon.*

*Love,
Mom*

*P.S. Okay, I'll give you a hint. It's filled with
love!*

The rectangular pouch was only about three inches
long and less than two inches wide. It was made of white
silk and embroidered with tiny, pink cherry blossoms.
At the top was a decorative bow and a drawstring made
of white cord. It was cute. A little weird. But cute.

Beneath the *omamori* was a shiny, bluish-gray square

of fabric. Gently, I lifted the kimono from its box. Silky folds parted to reveal a flock of hand-painted white cranes. Long, graceful necks fully outstretched and wingtips barely touching, the silver-trimmed birds soared across a steely sky. I had never owned anything this intricate or beautiful. It took me a while to get up the nerve to try it on, and when I finally did, it was much too big. The hem fell to my lower shins, and the wide bell sleeves came down several inches past my finger-tips. I had to wrap one side of the kimono nearly all the way around my waist to get the V to close in front. How much did my mother think I weighed? Dragging the long, matching sash behind me, I headed for the bath-room mirror. I wasn't sure how to tie the sash. Fawn would know.

Holding the neck in place, I touched a creamy crane gliding over the curve of my left shoulder. The blue-gray color was pretty, but it wasn't right for me. It made my hair look dull and my skin pasty.

I let go of the neck. The filmy fabric slipped to the floor. I hung the kimono on the only padded hanger in my closet. It looked strange floating next to my faded tees and ordinary hoodies. Like it did not belong here. Like it deserved better. I knew I would keep my mom's kimono forever. I also knew I would never put it on again.

Bringing the little silk *omamori* into my room, I laid it on one side of my pillow. Then I lay down beside it and did something I hardly ever did After Mom.

I cried.

Ten

"You did what?" Fawn nearly spit her sample of pomegranate-cranberry-lemonade on my shirt.

"I nominated Renata for fall court."

"Renata." She stared blankly at me. "Zickelfoos."

I drained my juice sample in one gulp and tried not to make a sour face. "Yep."

"Coco, have you lost your mind?" Fawn tossed her miniature white paper cup into the trash and rushed after my aunt.

Aunt Iona was about ten feet ahead of us, navigating her cart through the maze of other carts at the Costco warehouse. My dad worked on Saturdays. Aunt Iona didn't cook (she had a phobia of appliances catching fire), so she'd pick me up at the apartment and the two of us would go to Costco for lunch. We'd stroll around the warehouse snacking on store d'oeuvres—you know, the food samples the employees in the white coats and shower caps handed out. Whenever they could, Fawn and Adair came too. Adair couldn't make it today. She was attending her first cheerleading practice, thank you very much.

I caught up to Fawn. "Are you mad at me?"

"No."

She *was* mad. I could tell by her smooshed-in face.

"I thought you'd think it was a great idea, especially after how well things worked out for Adair, Willow, and Cadence."

"Yeah, what about that? You were only supposed to fix the score for Adair. *Adair*."

"You weren't in the gym during tryouts. You didn't see how great Willow and Cadence were. I couldn't leave them behind. They'd earned spots too."

"I'm sure they did great, but—"

"Girls!" My aunt was signaling to her right. "Peanut brittle!"

"Somebody is bound to figure it out," hissed Fawn, dodging a little boy. "And when they do . . ." She stopped to reach for a shard of peanut brittle. "Thank you," she said to the sample lady.

I was right behind her. "Thank you."

Two dark eyebrows hit the edge of a white shower cap. "Nobody ever says 'thank you.'"

"I wasn't stupid," I said in Fawn's right ear. "I made sure Dijon, Venice, Truffle, Évian, Lisbon, Stocklifter, and Geneva made the team. Of course, a few Somebodies had to go to make room. I figured Dover, Monaco, and Perrier were at the bottom of Dijon's food chain."

"Don't you see?" Fawn rapidly crunched the hard candy between her teeth. "You've raised their suspicions. If only one Nobody got through, Coach Notting and Miss Furdy would assume it was because of Mrs. Ignazio. But three Nobodies? That just doesn't happen. They're probably going over their judging sheets this minute."

"They aren't," I said, sucking on a shard of peanut brittle.

"They'll discover the scores were changed, and that'll be the end of us."

"They won't."

"It's doggie booties hell for us, for sure."

"Trust me." I touched her arm and enunciated very clearly. "They. Won't."

She frowned.

"Hey, look, soft tacos." I darted through the expressway of carts to get to the other side of the aisle.

Fawn caught my arm. "Coco?"

"What?"

She glared at me. "Why won't they figure it out?"

I could see she wasn't going to let this go. "Because they can't. See, the original sheets, uh . . . well, they sort of . . . Are you sure you want to know?"

"*What?*"

"Got shredded."

Fawn put two fingers to her lips. "You didn't."

"Me, personally? No."

"Then how?"

"I made a slight change to Coach Notting's instructions to Mrs. Rivkin."

I reached for a toothpick stuck through the middle of a little puffy tortilla triangle. "Thank you."

"You're welcome," said the lady.

"What did you do?" asked Fawn.

"I told her to shred the judging sheets once she was done tallying the scores."

Fawn let out a tiny cry.

Trailing my aunt's cart, Fawn and I finished our spicy beef soft tacos. We ate lobster puffs, chocolate muffins, candied pistachios, garlic noodles, and shrimp-and-pepper kabobs without saying a word to each other. Throwing away her mini kabob stick, Fawn finally spoke.

"There's no way Renata is going to beat Dijon for fall queen. You do know that, right?"

"I know. She could win one of the two princess crowns, though. Nobody really wants to vote for Venice." I mimicked the way Venice smacked her gum. *Snap. Snap. Snap.*

"What? You mean, you're not planning to hack into Mrs. Rivkin's computer and change the voting results?"

I gave her a sly smirk to tease her before I said, "No. Of course not. Look, I just want to give Renata a tiny taste of the cake Her Fabulousness and the Royal Court get to eat every day. Is that so awful?"

Fawn nibbled on a caramel-dipped apple slice. "I suppose not. But how?"

"I figured all we have to do is change her look a little."

"A little?"

"Okay, a lot. You could give her a fashion makeover and Adair could do something with her hair. I could help her with her speech—"

"It would take a miracle."

"Come on, Fawn, this is our chance to make our own footprints."

"Huh?"

"We could change Renata's life."

"Or destroy it. What if she loses and ends up hating us?"

"How could she hate us?" I teased. "We're very lovable girls."

"She has, like, a one percent chance of winning a princess crown."

"It's still a chance."

"You are relentless, you know that?"

"My aunt says it's one of my most annoying qualities. So will you do it?"

Fawn shook her head. "I guess so."

I threw an arm across her shoulders. "You're the best friend in the universe."

"I still think you've lost your mind."

"You could be right." I picked up the next sample and offered it to her. "Egg roll?"

"No, thanks." Fawn put a hand to her stomach. "Do they give out Pepto-Bismol or Tums samples anywhere?"

"I don't think so."

"They should. Right at the door as you go out. Or maybe as you come in." She grimaced. "Or both."

The edges of Fawn's face were starting to turn greenish yellow. I guess a pomegranate-cranberry-lemonade, spicy beef taco, lobster puff, chocolate muffin, candied pistachios, garlic noodles, shrimp-and-pepper kabob, egg roll lunch isn't for everybody.

"Does that mean you don't want to circle one more time?" I asked, popping the mini egg roll in my mouth.

Fawn burped. I took that as a no.

Eleven

13-22-44.

13-22-44.

I'd been chanting it in my head since I fell asleep last night. My dad was dropping me off at school very early—like "the rooster is still in REM sleep" early. I told him I was meeting Adair and Renata in the library to practice our presentation for leadership class. That much was true. Today each team was going to present its school improvement project idea. However, I didn't tell my dad that *before* I met up with my teammates, I had something else to do. It was the real reason I had to get to school at such a wicked hour.

I was on a top-secret mission.

13-22-44.

13-22-44.

Turning into the school driveway, my dad surveyed the nearly empty parking lot. He pulled up to the curb.

"It's awfully early. Are you sure the library is even open?"

"Uh-huh. Mrs. Dawkins is usually one of the first people here."

"Good luck today."

"Thanks." I ran my hand over my mom's *omamori*. I'd tied the little bag to the outside zipper of my sketchbook. "I'll need plenty of it to beat Dijon."

"All you can do is your best. And you've done that. Your design is terrific."

"Thanks." I looked through the windshield at the rising sun playing hide-and-seek between the fir trees. "I wish that was enough."

"Sometimes we have to accept that things are out of our hands."

"Aren't things only out of your hands if you put them down? Or never pick them up?"

He chuckled. "Good point, Coco Simone."

We both knew he used my middle name so he could say her name out loud. I didn't mind. I liked hearing it too.

"Say, I was thinking this Sunday we might go house hunting."

I bounced in my seat. "You mean . . . ?"

"It looks like we'll be staying for a while."

Yes! I could finally have a bedroom, one that I could paint any way I wanted. Most landlords (including the military) don't let you paint an apartment any color that isn't beige or beige related. But if we got our own place, I could paint angels or fairies or animals or anything on my walls. *My* walls. This was the best news ever!

My dad was sniffing the air. "Do you smell something funky?" He wrinkled his nose. "Did you bring home your gym clothes to wash?"

"Gotta fly, Dad." I yanked on the door handle. "Must be time for a new freshener in here. See ya." I leaped from the car with my sketchbook under my arm. Ripping open the back door, I grabbed my backpack off the backseat.

"Bye, Coco. Let me know how it—"

I'm sure he said "goes," but I didn't stick around long enough to find out.

Whew! That was close! If my dad only knew what was in my backpack. . . .

Miss Grace, our head janitor, was coming out of the building as I was going in. I held the door open for her so she could roll out her big garbage can on three wheels. "Thank you, Coco. Make it a great day."

"That's the idea," I said.

13-22-44.

13-22-44.

The magic numbers to open Dijon's door.

I kept repeating it as I sprinted through the empty hallways of Big Mess. I didn't dare bring Fawn's locker card with me to school, where it could be seen by a Somebody. Until a few days ago I had completely forgotten about it. The red card had been in my backpack pocket since that first day of school when Fawn had dropped it on her way out of the gym. All this time it had been there, patiently waiting for me to find it again. I suppose I should have thrown it away, but it would have been wrong to let such valuable, top-secret information go to waste, right?

My mission was simple: Get Fawn's locker back from Dijon. Fawn deserved to have her assigned locker back. Besides, three people in one locker was one person too many. Between Fawn's flute, Liezel's music, my art sketchbook, our coats, backpacks, notebooks, books, and lunches, you had to throw your whole body against the door to get the dumb thing to latch.

I headed to B wing to make a quick stop at my locker so I could drop off my coat and get my leadership notebook. Rounding the final corner, a humming noise made me pull up short. It sounded like a girl. . . .

Was that singing?

I knew it wasn't Miss Grace. I had already passed her going the opposite way. So who could it be at—I glanced at my watch—6:18 a.m.?

Hugging the wall, I peered around the corner.

Our locker was open. Liezel was in the middle of the hallway, playing air guitar to a song on her iPod. Two earbud wires swung in time to her strumming. She wasn't singing loudly, but her voice was on key, light, and angelic.

> *The only time you don't fight is when you sleep.*
> *The only time I don't cry is when you weep.*
> *You pretend to care,*
> *Tell me you'll always be there.*
> *And then you turn and go away. And then you go.*
> *Just go.*

Had she written it? It was probably on the CD she'd let me borrow. I should have listened to it. Feeling a sting of regret, I vowed to listen to it tonight.

I wonder what Her Fabulousness and the Royal Court would say if they could hear Liezel sing? I'd love to be a bug on Venice's pointy, black hat for that little discussion. No one—not even a Somebody—looks good in green.

My breath caught in my throat. The singing had stopped. I flattened my back against the wall. Our locker door slammed.

Go the other way! Please go the other way.

I strained for footsteps. I stayed glued to the wall, forcing myself to silently count to thirty. Liezel did not walk past. Slowly, I inched my face along the wall until I could just barely see around the corner. There was no sign of her, or anybody else. I raced to my locker, opened it, and exchanged my coat for my leadership notebook. I shut the door, bumping my shoulder against it as hard as I could, then I was off again, charging down the hall and taking the stairs two at a time. In sync with my chant, my backpack bounced against my spine.

13-22-44.

13-22-44.

At the top of the stairwell I glanced right. Then left. No one. My mission was going perfectly. So far.

I scurried to locker 229. The corner locker was easy to find, thanks to Dijon's heart-shaped beauty board Velcroed to the side. Stacking my stuff on the floor, I cracked my knuckles in preparation for the most difficult part of the operation. I spun the dial to the right to clear it, then lined up 13 with the red mark. My brain was whizzing at top speed. My fingers were icicles. My wrist was shaking so much, I had to hold my left hand under my elbow to steady it. I spun the knob left, passing 22 once, then stopping on it the second time around. Finally, I turned the dial to the right, to 44. This was it! I placed the metal handle between my thumb and index finger. And lifted. The door didn't open.

I jiggled the handle. Nothing. I jiggled harder. It wouldn't budge.

Had I gone too fast? Did I have the right combination? What if I'd memorized the wrong numbers? Or the right numbers in the wrong order?

A monster wave of fear rolled through me.

What should I do?

Try again?

Give up?

Every second I debated it increased my chances of getting caught.

You can do this. You have to do this.

For Fawn. For all the Nobodies.

I shook out my arms to get some feeling back in my fingertips. I twirled the dial five times to the right to be absolutely sure I cleared it, then inched the 13 up to the red vertical mark.

Keep going. Calm. Calm. Calm.

I turned the knob to the left, passing 22 once, then ever so carefully sneaking up on it on the second time around.

One more. You're almost there.

I nudged the knob twenty-two clicks to the right. This was it—44. I rubbed my fingertips together.

Coco Sherwood, if you ever had any magic in you. . . .

"Abracadabra," I whispered, reaching for the handle.

"*What* do you think you're doing?"

Twelve

I whipped around. "Évian!"

Tipping her head, she wriggled her fingers at me.

"So what *am* I doing? What am *I* doing?" With one foot I scooted my backpack behind me. "Well, I . . . um . . . actually, I was just, uh . . ."

"Yes?"

"I was about to . . . Well, I mean . . . I was thinking of . . ."

"Uh-huh?"

By her mocking grin, it was clear she was loving my misery.

I couldn't turn to mist now. I was going to have to tell her the truth and beg for mercy. The odds of me getting any weren't good. The Royal Court never cut anybody an inch of slack. I had a vision of myself hanging upside down from the flag pole out front below the big St. Bernard pennant.

I dropped my arms in surrender. "Okay, Évian, here's the thing. See, I was going to—"

"Coco!"

We heard the squeal of rubber sliding across waxed linoleum. A flash of brown turned the corner and barreled toward us.

My jaw fell. "Liezel?"

"Sorry it took so long." She huffed, holding out a pen to me.

Hesitantly, I took it. "Oh, uh . . . thanks."

Liezel turned to Évian. "Do you need a pen too?"

Évian's forehead crinkled with suspicion. "Why?"

"To write down Dijon's favorite blush color," said Liezel, moving toward the beauty board. "Coco's pen ran out of ink, and I didn't have one, so I ran down to our locker to get another one and . . . uh . . . here we are. Flamingo Pink. Number Nine." Liezel elbowed me. Hard.

I sprang into action, flipping through my leadership notebook to find a blank page. I began to copy Dijon's beauty board.

"We have to write it down before she puts up a new message," said Liezel. "Do you know what it's going to be?"

"No," said Évian cautiously. "She doesn't tell me."

"Really? That's too bad."

Évian shifted from one foot to the other, then back again. I heard her ankle pop. Without another word to us, she turned and walked away. She took her time about it, though.

I kept writing, sneaking a glance or two at Évian out of the corner of my eye. Évian James was a bit of a mystery. I had never heard her say the ugly things that came so easily to Dijon, Venice, and Truffle. But she didn't stick up for people either. Silence was no excuse. The way I saw it, she was one of *them* until she proved she wasn't. I didn't put the pen down until we heard the exit door clang shut. "Thanks, Liezel. Do you think she'll tell?"

"I'll bet you a slice of pepperoni she already has."

I kicked my backpack. "Shoot!"

"Coco, what's going on?"

I liked Liezel, but I wasn't convinced I could trust her. Not yet.

"I did save you, you know," pressed Liezel. "The least you could do is tell me why."

"You really want to know? Because once I tell you, you're involved up to your eyeballs—"

"I can handle it."

"Okay," I said, dragging my backpack toward us by the left strap. "Stand back."

Liezel chuckled. "Is it going to explode or something?"

"Technically, no." I unzipped an outside pocket and, with two fingers, lifted out a limp, charcoal-black, L-shaped blob.

"Pee ewww!" Waving a hand in front of her face, Liezel took a full step back. "What is it?"

Tears sprang to my eyes. "It used to be my dad's old, white crew sock. It's been marinating in the condo compost bin all week." Suspended in the air, the sock was shedding bits of dirt, leaves, and a fettuccini noodle (or earthworm—hard to tell).

Liezel held her nose. "*That* is gross."

"I call it Operation Locker Rescue. I was going to put this in the locker to smell it up, so Dijon and her friends would move out—"

"And Fawn could move back in," Liezel finished, her voice nasal. "If I were you, Coco, I wouldn't put it in her locker—"

"Because Évian will tell Dijon."

"No."

"Because it's a horrible thing to do to somebody, even if she is a complete pain."

"No, I—"

"You're right. Of course you're right. I don't know what I was thinking. I was just trying—"

"Coco!"

"What?"

"I meant you should put it *under* her locker. See that space at the bottom? She'll smell it, all right, but she won't know where it's coming from. It'll drive her bananas."

"Ohhhh. Good plan. Have you done this before?"

Liezel snickered, but she didn't say no.

"Like this?" Squatting, I stuffed the sock into the small slit between the bottom of the locker and the floor. I used the pen to push it as far back as I could.

"Perfect," said Liezel.

I stood up. The odor was wafting up through the little vents in the front of the locker. With each second that passed, the stench was becoming more powerful.

"I can't wait to see what you've got in mind for the next phase," said my locker partner.

"Next phase?" I shuddered. "You think I'll need one?"

"You might. Maybe even a Phase Three. After all, we are talking about Dijon and her friends here. They're not going to go quietly."

I stroked my chin. "I'll have to think about it. I'll need something even stinkier than socks for Phase Two, but what could be worse than—"

I was interrupted by the slam of a locker in F wing.

"We need to get out of here," whispered Liezel.

I put a hand on her arm. "Fawn doesn't know anything about this."

"Got it. We have to split up. Where are you headed?"

"Library."

"Right. You go that way. I'll go this way." Liezel bounded toward the stairs. Before she made the turn, she called out, "Smell you later."

I laughed, picking up my backpack. I should have followed Liezel's advice and taken off in the other direction, but I didn't. I couldn't. Not yet.

I had to find out one thing. Despite the risk, I had to do it.

I glanced right, then left, to be absolutely sure I was alone. Oh so gently, I placed my thumb and index finger on the handle of locker 229. And lifted.

Poof!

The door opened.

Thirteen

Renata was behind Adair.

I was behind Renata.

The three of us were mere steps from Mr. Tanori's classroom.

Adair glanced back. "Let me hear it, girls," she cried, holding up a fist. "Pumped and ready?"

"Pumped and ready," I echoed.

"Maybe we could practice one more time," said Renata before a giant sneeze erupted from her ruddy face. "Rachoo!"

"Bless you," said Adair, leaning over to shoot me a worried look.

We'd decided Renata should do the biggest chunk of the presentation. Well, Adair and I had decided. Renata didn't want to do it. I knew she was afraid she'd lisp. But the project was her idea, and it seemed only right she be the one to talk about it. Once Renata was done discussing how painting a mural over the ugly, orange wall in the cafeteria would boost school spirit and make a difference in our pathetic world, Adair would share the details, like how long it would take to paint it (around a month, we figured) and how much it would cost to buy primer, paint, and supplies (about a thousand dollars). We'd even gotten Mrs. Wyndham, the art teacher, to agree to give art students extra credit for helping to paint the mural.

Lastly, I would reveal my design. Ta-da! My drawing was a collage of twenty-two faces (one face for each year the school had existed) intertwined with swirling grapevines and leaves. I was going through a Celtic art phase. The prickly vines represented our school, Briar Green, and the faces, of course, were meant to symbolize students. I'd incorporated our school colors into the pencil sketch, using muted shades of green and silvery-blue to create a serene yet spooky mood. Many of the faces were easy to spot among the winding tendrils, but others were almost impossible to find. None was recognizable, of course. Still, if you looked hard enough, you could find Liezel's brooding eyes, Fawn's bent silhouette, Adair's giggle dimples, and Dijon's scorning mouth. I didn't know why I'd put Dijon in the mural. I guess everything you experience can inspire you, even the bad stuff. Especially the bad stuff.

I didn't have any illusions about the outcome of all my hard work. Everybody knew Dijon's idea—however outrageous, impractical, or costly—was going to win by a landslide. That's how things were done in the kingdom of Big Mess. Yet, I couldn't seem to stop the war of hope within me. My brain shouted, "Forget it, forget, forget it!" even as my heart beat, "Imagine it, imagine it, imagine it."

Dijon stalked into class with Truffle and Venice in her boot prints.

"I'm telling you I didn't put anything in it," said Truffle.

"There has to be some reason why it smells like something died in there," said Dijon.

I muffled a snort.

"It wasn't me," insisted Truffle. "Maybe Venice—"

"Don't even go there," said Venice, gnashing her gum. "You probably stepped in dog doo again."

"I did not." Truffle quickly checked the soles of her shoes.

Venice sighed. "If anyone can find poop, Truff, it's you."

"Yeah? What about you?"

"Me?"

"You and your random farts of blindness."

A small giggle may have escaped my lips.

Venice's head did an owl-like spin. "Shut up, Cuckoo. Nobody's talking to you." She was really wailing on her gum.

Snap. Snap. Snap.

Supreme! Operation Locker Rescue was working better than I'd ever anticipated. This squabbling among the Royal Court was a juicy bonus.

Venice turned back to Truffle. "Get your stuff out of our locker by noon today."

"You can't throw me out. It's Dijon's locker. Only Dijon can throw me out."

Dijon slipped a twisted cord of red licorice out of her mouth and said coolly, "Get out."

"But, Dij—"

"And, Venice, get that locker cleaned out by this afternoon."

Venice said, "Yes, my queen." Or something to that effect.

I could hardly wait to text Liezel.

As Mr. Tanori took roll, Renata played her invisible

piano with more determination than ever. Fingers were flying back and forth across her desk. I wondered what she was playing. Was it anything I knew? Was it hard?

"Are you sure she can do this?" Adair hissed across the aisle.

"If she has a problem, we'll help her."

"If she has a problem, *we* have a problem. We'll get the D too."

"Nobody's getting a D," I said with a lot more confidence than I felt.

Mr. Tanori asked which group wanted to go first. Dijon flicked her finger against Venice's shoulder blade. Venice's hand went up. But it wasn't fast enough. Our teacher had already picked Cord Nagel. Cord was a Sortabody hotshot basketball player, so, of course, Cord's group wanted to buy new basketballs and hoops for the gym.

Yawnfest.

I was awakened by lackluster applause.

"Which group would like to be next?" asked Mr. Tanori.

Determined not to be overlooked, or maybe because she didn't want to endure any more of Dijon's flicking fingernails, Venice flew out of her chair.

"Good enthusiasm," said Mr. Tanori. "Dijon, Venice, Truffle, and Breck. You're up."

We were about to see the main attraction, so, naturally, the applause got louder. Some of the guys whistled. With a quick curtsy Dijon pranced to take a spot in the front of the room. Venice, Truffle, and Breck stood off to the side. Venice held a rolled-up poster. She kept snapping the rubber band around it. *Zing! Zing!* Dijon gave her a dirty look. She stopped.

Dijon put a hand on her slim hip. She was wearing a tangerine-colored T-shirt that read DON'T HATE ME BECAUSE I'M CUTE. HATE ME BECAUSE I'M RICHER THAN YOU. "Is everybody ready? Todd, shut up." Dijon let out a giggle. "Okay, my fabulous idea is to paint a mural over the pukey orange wall in the cafeteria."

For the next several minutes the only thing I could process was sound.

Whap! Adair's hands hitting her cheeks.

Wonk! Renata's forehead hitting her desk.

Wang! My sketchbook hitting the floor.

When, finally, all of my senses returned, Venice and Truffle were unrolling the poster. It was an acrylic painting of a St. Bernard. At least, I think it was a dog. The animal was drawn completely out of proportion. A malnourished body supported an enormous head with a pair of Chihuahua-sized ears. It looked like some kind of freakish creature Dr. Frankenstein might piece together so his monster could have a pet. Below the creepy dog were our school shield and a banner that read BRIAR GREEN ST. BENERD PRIDE! Yes, "Bernard" was misspelled. Dijon had signed the lower right-hand corner of the poster. Her name was twice the size of the banner. No one else's name was on the poster.

"Isn't it fabulous?" Dijon beckoned to the class, signaling the time had come for her subjects to give her plenty of praise.

Ew.

"Oh, yeah!" Parker let out a whistle.

"Awesome idea," said Todd.

"Wicked design, Dijon."

As she left, Dijon blew kisses to the class.

Double ew.

Adair leaned across the aisle. "What do we do?"

"Let another group go first. When it's our turn, we'll pretend it's no big deal that we both had the same idea."

"That could be a problem." Adair was glancing toward the back.

Behind us, one row over, Renata was pulling up the cowled collar of her pink-and-white sweater over her head. She looked like a candy-cane-striped turtle.

I waved. "Renata, it's okay."

"Yes, Coco," said Mr. Tanori, motioning to me. "Have your group come on up."

"Oh no, Mr. Tanori, I wasn't—"

"Next we have Coco, Adair, and Renata," said our teacher, stepping aside.

Pulling a pretend noose around her neck, Adair stuck her tongue out. We were both thinking the same thing. We might as well get it over with as quickly as possible. Holding my sketchbook to my chest, I followed Adair to the front. When we turned around, Renata wasn't with us. She was still at her desk, still hiding out in her Christmas-themed turtle shell. She had slumped down her seat. Way down. The ends of her oversize sleeves flopped back and forth—two flags in surrender.

"Miss Zickelfoos?" Mr. Tanori called. "Join your team, please."

Renata melted out of her chair. By the time she reached us, most of her head had emerged from her sweater. However, the thick collar still clung to her chin.

Dijon, Venice, and Truffle had their heads together. Unzipping my sketchbook, I turned to Renata and gave her a supportive smile. "You'll be okay. Once you start talking, it will get easier."

Pushing up her red glasses, Renata took a big breath. Then she turned to face the class. "Hi, everyone. Uh . . . our idea . . . ith . . ." Her voice teetered. "Well, it'th kind of like . . ."

"We can't hear you!" Parker yelled from the back of the room.

She cleared her throat and tried again. "Um . . . we came up with . . . I mean, it'th thort of like . . ."

"Come on, Renata Piñata," called Venice. "Thpit it out already."

"What's wrong?" Dijon slowly tapped four turquoise nails against her desk. "Sweater got your tongue?"

The class laughed. Truffle nearly fell out of her chair.

I could feel my blood starting to warm. My arms tightened around my sketchbook.

"Quiet," said Mr. Tanori firmly. "We listen to one another with respect and courtesy in this class. Is that clear?"

"Yes, of course," said Dijon sweetly. "Go ahead, Renata. Continue with your *totally* original idea."

Renata began twirling her sleeves. "Um . . . well, it'th not exactly original. . . . I mean . . . I thought it wath at the time, but now . . ."

If only I could sprinkle some of my glitter over her or extend my force field to cover her. But I could do nothing. It had to be her. It had to be *all* her.

Come on, Renata. You can do it. This is your moment to show them you are so much more than they think you are. Don't worry about lisping. JUST START.

"I . . . I . . . can't." That's as far as Renata got before she bolted for the hallway. She did, however, manage to utter one complete thought as she flung open the door. "I'm thorry."

We knew what she meant.

Fourteen

"Mr. Tanori, can I . . . ?"

A pink slip of paper appeared.

I had never loved a teacher more than I did Mr. Tanori at that moment. Crumpling the hall pass in my fist, I ran for the one place I knew I'd escape to if I ever freaked out in class: the girls' bathroom down the hall. Cracking open the outer door, I called out gently, "Renata?"

No answer.

I went inside and peeked in every stall. No Renata. I tried the bathroom in C wing. She wasn't there, either. I ran upstairs to check the girls' bathrooms in D and E wings. Nothing.

Where on earth could she be? She wouldn't leave campus, would she?

Come on, Coco, think. THINK.

Winded from my wild dash around Big Mess, I leaned

against the wall outside the science labs. I closed my eyes and pretended to push a pair of red glasses up my nose.

I'm Renata Zickelfoos. I'm wearing my favorite pink-and-white-striped sweater with a long blue scarf wrapped around my neck. I'm feeling humiliated and frustrated. I need a safe place to go, somewhere I can feel completely comfortable, somewhere I can release my pain without anybody around to—

I opened my eyes. I knew where Renata was.

Tearing down the stairs, I jogged the entire length of A wing. I flew past the chorus room, the band room, and the instrument storage room to the end of the hallway, where three music practice rooms were clustered in a semicircle. The door to each room had a tiny window. Each window was dark. Shoot!

I turned the handle of the first door. It was locked. I moved to the middle door. Also locked. Desperate, I grabbed for the last doorknob.

Please let her be here.

The door easily unlatched.

"Renata?"

A dark figure was hunched over a piano. A circular window above the piano let in just enough light for me to make out the outline of flying saucer hair.

"I told you I didn't want to do it," said a husky voice.

An old, upright piano took up two-thirds of the tiny room, so there was barely enough space for me to shut the door and turn around. "It wasn't your fault, Renata. Who knew Dijon would come up with the same idea? Of course, torturing you with it was just a bonus. . . ." I tried to let out a light laugh, but it was too loud for the claustrophobic room.

Renata ran her fingertips over the black piano keys. She did not press them down, and, for the first time, I wondered if she really knew how to play the piano. Maybe all she ever did was practice on her invisible keys. Maybe she'd never played a note in her life. It made me sad to think the only thing Renata might be good at was nothing more than an illusion.

Not that I could condemn her. I was the master of illusions.

I slid in beside her on the tippy piano bench, prepared to stay as long as it took.

"Coco, you're pretty smart. Can I ask you something?"

"Sure, but I should tell you, Adair and Fawn are much smarter than I. Or is it 'me'? No, I think it's 'I.' Told you I'm not that smart."

"Why do you like to do that?"

"Do what?"

"Pretend to be worse than you are."

That startled me. And it bothered me. Why would I *like* to do that? Why would anybody deliberately want to be less than what they were? Renata Zickelfoos wasn't one of my friends. She didn't know me. She didn't know anything about me. "Maybe I should go," I said, my voice frosty.

"I'm sorry. I always say the wrong thing. Stay, Coco. Please stay."

I could hear the desperation in her voice. She was one syllable away from crying. "Okay," I said.

Renata's fingers curled. "Every time I get the chance to do something where I can prove myself, I screw it up. Every time. Why do I do that?"

How do you answer a question like that?

"I don't know," I said. "If you think you're going to fail, though, you probably will."

Renata sighed. "I don't fit in here. It's like this place is a big jigsaw puzzle of . . . of . . . the desert or something, and I'm the one piece that goes to a totally different puzzle, you know? Like I belong to the forest puzzle or some completely different picture. Someone like you probably has no clue what I'm talking about."

"Oh, really? I've felt that way at pretty much every school I've ever been to. And I've been to *a lot* of schools."

"You have?"

"Five in seven years. I never had any friends, either. I used to sit on the playground or in the cafeteria alone and draw. It wasn't until I came here that things were different."

"So what changed?"

"Adair and Fawn. They talked to me on my first day here." But even as I said it, I knew it was more than that. I knew I had something to do with it too. "And I guess I got tired of hiding. I *know* I was tired of being alone. I was ready to look up from my sketchbook."

"You make it sound simple."

I sighed. "Nothing about friendship is simple."

Renata took a piece of paper out of the back pocket of her jeans. She slowly unfolded it and held it out to me. "Mrs. Rivkin gave this to me this morning."

In the dim light I couldn't read it. I looked to her for help.

"It's a letter from the ASB. It says I've been nominated for fall court."

I tried to act casual, but inside I was leaping for joy. "That's incredible."

"It's impossible. It's a joke, Coco. It has to be."

It had never occurred to me she would take the nomination as a prank. But what other way could she possibly take it? Teasing was all Renata knew.

"It *doesn't* have to be," I said.

"What do you mean?"

"What difference does it make how it was intended? Now it's yours. You can make it whatever you want. We could help you—Fawn, Adair, Liezel, and me."

"You're saying I should do it?" She snorted. "Me, Renata Piñata, should run for fall court?"

"Yeah, you're probably right. Why bother to change now? We've only got almost *five* more years until graduation. You can hold on that long."

Renata didn't say anything, and that worried me. She was probably talking herself right back into that pink-and-white-striped turtle shell of hers. I was starting to feel confident we could manage to whip up a little magic on the outside. But she had to do the real work. Renata had to *want* to be free.

"Come on, Ren," I said softly. "Take a chance. Look up."

Renata hit middle C with her index finger. The note

rang out strongly, then faded away. She waited until the room was silent again to say, "Okay."

"Good. I'll text Fawn and Adair—"

"Oh, God, Adair!" She covered her mouth. "She probably hates my guts. What happened after I ran away? Did we get an F in leadership?"

"I don't think so. But if we did, we did."

For the first time since I'd entered the practice room, Renata looked at me. As she did, a beam of light from the little round window passed between us. The sun made her rectangular glasses glow lava red, turning lifeless brown eyes into honey-colored marbles. I could almost see through them. Or maybe they were seeing through me.

"Coco, just so you know," she said, placing her fingers on the keys again, "if you ever had to run, I'd come after you."

I didn't tell her that was one of the sweetest things anyone had ever said to me.

But I think she knew.

Fifteen

Fawn's eyes were growing by the second. "So did you guys fail?"

"Not yet," said Adair, ripping open the Velcro flap of her purple nylon lunch bag with more force than was necessary. She took out a sandwich bag filled with split carrots and celery. "Mr. Tanori is giving us a do-over on Friday. I hope Renata doesn't choke again. We're not going to get a third chance."

"She won't," I said, popping the top off my salad.

"She'll feel a lot more confident after her makeover tomorrow," said Fawn. She pointed a soft pretzel stick at us. "Don't forget. My house. Four o'clock."

"I'm there," I said. I opened the little packet of Italian dressing that came with my salad and squeezed some of the oil onto my lettuce.

"Me too," said Liezel.

"Adair?"

"Huh?" Adair was staring at Her Fabulousness and the Royal Court. She was making a T out of two carrot sticks. I did a double-take. Was she signaling to them? "Are you coming to my house after school tomorrow to do Renata's hair?"

"Uh-huh," Adair said.

"I'll let her go through my closet and see what fits," said Fawn. "She's taller than me. I might have to do some sewing. She likes scarves, so I was thinking maybe my light blue pashmina with the sparkly stars and my black harem pants. They're pretty long. What do you think, Adair?"

"It's fine," she said flatly. "None of it matters, you know. She isn't going to win."

"Nobody expects her to," I said, spearing a couple of pieces of limp lettuce.

"Then what's the point?"

Unbelievable!

After all that she had endured to reach her goal, Adair, more than anyone, should have understood what we were trying to achieve.

"Isn't it obvious?" I said, throwing my hands into the air. "The point is growing. The point is dreaming. The point is *becoming*! Haven't you ever gone after something you wanted, even when you knew the odds were against you?"

We all knew what I was talking about, and if Adair would have simply said that one little word we were all expecting to hear, the whole thing would have ended there. But she didn't and so, unfortunately, it didn't.

"Oh, Coco, you're being overdramatic."

"I'd rather be overdramatic than cruel."

"Cruel!" Adair gasped. "I'm trying to *save* Renata from embarrassing herself in front of the whole school the way she did today in leadership—"

"She didn't embarrass herself," I interrupted.

"What do you call a meltdown in front of the entire class?"

"You'd have freaked out too if somebody had swiped your idea."

"*What?*"

I hadn't meant to say it—not yet, anyway—but a thought had been simmering in my head since my talk with Renata. A lot of little things were beginning to add up to one very big thing.

"I know you're going to think I'm nuts," I said, "but I'm pretty sure Dijon's group stole our project idea."

"Why would you think something like that?"

"Exhibit A: When has Dijon ever volunteered for anything? She's all about playing the game and making people wait on her. But *this* time, she was practically stabbing Venice with her fingernails to get their group up first. Why? Because they knew that in order for them to look like geniuses and for us to look like idiots, they'd have to give their presentation *before* we did. Exhibit B: When it was our turn, Her Fabulousness made fun of Renata, then she pretended to apologize and said, 'Go ahead with your totally original idea.' '*Totally original idea*'? Come on! That was a deliberate taunt. It was as if she knew what we were going to say before we said it." I sat back. My work here was done.

"You're absolutely right, Coco," said Adair, giving me a thin strand of hope.

"I am?"

"I think you're nuts."

The strand broke.

"Okay," said Adair, nibbling on a stick of celery. "For the sake of argument, *how* did they steal our idea?"

"Uh . . . well, that's the part I haven't quite figured out yet."

"You shouldn't go around accusing people unless you're sure."

My head started to tighten. "What does it matter how they did it? Maybe Her Fabulousness overheard us practicing in the library. Maybe one of the Royal Court saw my sketchbook. Maybe someone ac—" I froze.

Did I dare say it?

"What did someone ax?" asked Liezel.

I was glad she misinterpreted. "Never mind."

"Is that all you're going to eat for lunch, Adair?" asked Fawn, staring at Adair's bag of veggies. "You want some of my sauerkraut?" She opened a plastic bowl, and the smell—a cross between vinegar and dirty diapers— hit us like teargas. My eyes started watering.

"Yow," said Liezel, pulling back.

"Oh my God," cried Adair.

"I know it smells pretty wonky," said Fawn, "but it tastes good. It's just pickled cabbage—"

Adair spun to face me. "You!"

"Me? I hate sauerkraut—"

"You think I told Dijon about our idea, don't you?"

My mouth said no, but my head bobbed yes. Stupid head. "I'm not saying you did it on purpose. Maybe you were talking to Her Fabulousness and the Royal Court at cheer practice, and it slipped out—"

"Maybe you're delusional. And you really need to stop calling them that."

"What?"

"Her Fabulousness and the Royal Court. It's pretty rude."

"You never thought it was rude before. Last year you thought it was funny." Crunching a crouton, I muttered, "Two weeks on cheer staff, and you're morphing into one of them."

"Ah!" She flung a celery stick at me. It hit my neck. For such a bland vegetable, celery sure could sting. "If you only knew how many times I've defended you to them."

"You defended *me*?" I clutched my heart. "Oh, thank you, thank you, Adair. I don't know what I'd do if Dijon and Venice didn't like me."

"That's right, I forgot. You don't need anybody, do you?"

Fawn threw her hands up. "Stop, you guys, before someone says—"

"Coco, I've got a news flash for you," growled Adair. "You're not nearly as tough as you think you are."

"And you're not nearly as popular as you think you are."

She narrowed her eyes. "What's that supposed to mean?"

I opened my mouth, but Fawn got there first. Thank goodness, she got there first. "Nothing," snapped Fawn. "She didn't mean anything."

"No, she meant something, all right. If there's one thing about Coco, it's that she always means something." Adair turned to me. "You think all I want is to be popular, is that it? If that were true, I'd be over there eating lunch with Dijon and her friends right now, because they invited me, you know—"

"I wouldn't want to hold you back. Feel free to go any time you want." I stabbed a plump cherry tomato with my spork. The tomato burst, squirting juice all over the front of my T-shirt and the sleeve of Adair's white, crocheted cardigan.

"Eeek!" she screamed.

"Oops," I said with a snicker.

Adair was not amused. "You did that on purpose!"

"I didn't. Honestly, Adair. It was an acci—"

"This isn't even my sweater," said Adair, untangling herself from the bench we shared. "It's Truffle's."

Fawn's eyebrows went up. "Truffle's?"

"She wanted to wear my denim jacket, so we swapped.

If you've ruined this, Coco, I'm going to have to pay for it."

"You won't. It's not ruined." I reached for a couple of napkins. "It's only a little tomato juice. It'll wash out. I'm sorry, Adair, really, I am." I held the napkins out to her, but she refused to take them.

Adair quickly gathered her stuff. "I'll be back," she said as she stomped away, but I knew she wouldn't. She had taken everything with her.

"It really wasn't on purpose," I pleaded with Fawn and Liezel.

"We know," said Liezel.

"It'll be okay," said Fawn, but the look on her face said otherwise.

Adair crossed the cafeteria, her blond hair streaming out in determined waves behind her. She was almost to the door when she stopped, or something stopped her. I couldn't tell. A bunch of boys were blocking my view, so it took me a few minutes to see she was talking to . . . to . . .

Truffle and Stocklifter.

Über-ew.

Adair pointed to the tomato juice spots dotting the sweater, then over to me. Truffle shook her head. It was weird seeing Truffle in Adair's jacket, and not just because the arms were too long. I knew that faded jacket as well as I knew its owner. The tip of the left collar never stayed down. The right cuff was missing a rivet. There was a tiny black swish near the left hip that had happened last summer when Adair had laughed so hard at my imitation of a frog, she'd dropped her Sharpie pen. Adair's beloved jacket didn't belong on Truffle.

Stocklifter stole a napkin from Dover and gave it to Adair so she could dab the spots on her sweater. A few minutes later Adair left the cafeteria with Truffle and Stock.

A tremor rocketed up my spine. It hadn't taken Adair long to ditch her Nobody friends for the Somebodies, had it? If that's what she wanted, then she deserved every spiteful thing Her Fabulousness and the Royal Court were about to heap on her.

No, she didn't. Not really.

I was mad. She was mad. We would both calm down and make up.

Wouldn't we?

Fawn was gathering up her trash. I watched her place the lid back on the plastic bowl. "Could I have that?" I asked.

"My sauerkraut? Uh, yeah, sure." Slightly confused, Fawn slid the bowl toward me. "Enjoy."

When Fawn went to dump her stuff in the garbage, I turned to Liezel. We were in a public place, so I couldn't say anything. Instead, I held up two fingers and wiggled them. It took Liezel a few seconds to catch on.

When she did, her lips slid up the right side of her face. "Perfect."

Sixteen

"Above the eyes or below?" I asked.

"Just above," said Fawn on my right side.

"Agreed," said Liezel on my left. "But don't go above the eyebrows. She'll look like we stuck a bowl on her head and cut around it."

"Straight across or angled?"

"Slightly angled," said Fawn after a moment of thought.

"Agreed," said Liezel. "But don't overdo it. She'll look like she's got a lopsided head."

"Thick or wispy?"

"Somebody cut!" came the cry from behind a reddish-brown curtain of bangs.

"Okay," I said meekly.

I'd stalled as long as I could. Adair was almost an hour late. She probably wasn't coming. We had barely spoken since our fight yesterday, and today she had eaten lunch with *them*. I had tried to pretend it didn't bother me. But, of course, it had.

I picked up the scissors from Fawn's dresser. Sliding a section of hair between my fingers, I made the first diagonal cut a few inches beneath the bridge of her nose. The room fell silent and stayed that way as I continued across the width of her bangs. We all let out a sigh of relief when I clipped the last section. Using the very tips of the scissors, I cut a fraction of an inch up into the line of bangs to fringe the edges the way I'd watched stylists do hundreds of times only a few inches in front of my own face.

"Look, Renata, you have eyes!" said Liezel.

"We should trim the ends, too," said Fawn.

"Agreed," said Liezel.

I liked how everyone kept using the word "we," even though I was the one taking all the risks. Sure, I snipped my bangs all the time, but I'd never cut someone else's. If you do something to your own hair, oh well, you cover it with a hairband or something, but do something awful to someone else's hair, and you've made an enemy for life.

Was it getting hot in here or was it just the color of Fawn's room? I'd never been inside a sunset before, but I bet it would be like Fawn's bedroom. Every wall was painted a different vibrant shade of the horizon. Orange to the north. Red to the east. Pink to the west. Purple to the south. I loved it! Fawn's sewing machine and bookshelf, crammed with rolls of fabric, took up the orange wall. The pink wall was papered with dozens of fashion spreads she'd ripped out of *Teen Vogue*, *Seventeen*, and other magazines. She had plenty of her own sketches tacked to the wall too. Some had little squares of fabrics pinned next to them. When Dad and I got our house, I was going to paint murals on my walls and decorate them with sketches too.

I swiveled Renata's chair so she faced the mirror above Fawn's dresser. Brushed out, Renata's hair fell about five inches past her shoulders. The layered ends were dry and split. "Shoulders or collarbone?" I asked.

"Collarbone," said Fawn.

"Agreed," said Liezel.

Renata made a mousy squeak, but didn't protest. I cut a little at a time so I wouldn't freak her out. Or myself.

Fawn flopped on her bed with her phone. "I just got a text from Adair."

"Where is she?" asked Liezel. "When is she coming?"

"Let's see . . . it says, 'Stuck at cheer practice.'" Fawn sighed. "She's not coming."

Cheer this. Cheer that. I was getting a little tired of hearing the "ch" word.

"Ever since she joined ch—the squad"—I caught myself—"she's not the same person."

"How could she be?" asked Renata. "Everything's different for her now."

That stung, but I knew she was right. And I knew it was my fault. By changing the cheer scores, I had given Adair everything she'd always wanted. Unfortunately, I had also blurred the lines of social order at Big Mess. I had opened the door between their world and ours. How could I possibly stop Adair if she chose to walk through it?

"I'm scared about our presentation," said Renata, never taking her eyes off the path of my scissors. "It's so much pressure. Whenever I have to speak in public, I start lisping. I get so nervous, I feel like I'm going to pass out."

"Wiggle your fingers and toes," I said. "It helps keep blood flowing and releases nervous energy."

"You should hum a song," said Fawn, still on her back. "It'll relax you and warm up your voice."

"Find a friendly face in the audience to talk to,"

added Liezel. "And be honest. Audiences like honesty. They also like it when they get to participate, so include them in your talk."

"So let me get this straight," Renata said. "I should wiggle around, hum a tune, tell everyone I'm going to lisp, then faint, and ask them to catch me?"

We laughed—Fawn most of all. She fell off the bed and onto my backpack. "Ow!" she said, rubbing her lower back. "What have you got in there?" She unzipped the pocket. "Oh, it's a CD."

"That's Liezel's band," I said sheepishly. I still hadn't listened to her CD.

"Can we play it?"

With an uncertain grin Liezel gave permission.

Fawn slid the disc into her laptop. Hearing Liezel's voice on speakers was weird, but a good weird. Her voice was as pure and beautiful as it had been in the hallway at Big Mess, maybe even better with the band.

"This is good!" I shouted to Liezel above the music.

"This is *great*," called Fawn, hopping up to dance around her room. My friend Fawn is an amazing designer. She is an amazing student. But she is not— not even remotely—an amazing dancer.

I lowered the scissors. I was done. It was a simple cut:

straight across, and a hair below the tops of the shoulders (ha! I just got that), with angled bangs she could pull forward or tuck back into a barrette. It was all I knew how to do. But it made a stark difference. Now you could see her slightly concaved cheekbones, oval face, and long neck. Step back, people! Renata Zickelfoos had a neck. Believe me, when she'd unwrapped that scarf of hers, I had been prepared for the worst—a big lump, a hairy wart, a mole the size of Montana. But no! Not a single lump, wart, or mole to be found.

Renata turned left and right, studying herself in the mirror. Little furrows appeared on her forehead. Uh-oh. Was she going to cry? Had I done that horrible of a job? I started to reach for the box of tissues when she whispered, "I like it."

"Me too," said Liezel.

Fawn patted my back and whispered, "Adair couldn't have done any better."

Oh yes, she could have, but remembering Renata's minilecture, I gritted my teeth and absorbed the praise. "Thanks."

"Come on, Renata, let's go raid my stuff," said Fawn, leading the way into her mammoth walk-in closet. "Let's start with tops."

While the two of them picked out clothes, Liezel and I lay on Fawn's bed. We listened to a few more songs from Avalanche and flipped through last year's yearbook. The yearbooks were all presold by the time I'd gotten to Big Mess, so I hadn't gotten to buy one. We laughed at the faculty section. True to form, Waffles was crooked and Coach Notting growled at the camera. Liezel and I took our time going through the seventh-grade mug shots. Considering I'd only been going to Big Mess since last spring, I knew a lot of people. What I didn't realize until I saw them all together was that there were *so* many Nobodies. They were all lined up in precise rows. Row after row after row of nice, neat, never-make-trouble Nobodies.

Not long ago you could have pasted my picture on the end of any row on any page. But not anymore. Now I was on a mission to give back what the Somebodies had taken away. Insult by insult. Glare by glare. Cackle by cackle. I even had a trusty assistant.

"Nice work, today," I said, raising my arm. I turned my palm out.

Liezel slapped my hand. "Right back at ya, partner."

We were, of course, referring to Phase Two of Operation Locker Rescue. After school Liezel had acted as lookout while I'd poured some of Fawn's toxic sauerkraut in the slot under Dijon's locker (I didn't need much!). It had taken less than ten seconds to complete our task, though I had lingered longer at Dijon's locker than I should have. It was that beauty board, that condescending, puffed-up pink heart of a dry-erase board that was Dijon's mouthpiece. I hated the thing. I hated everything about it, from its lacy pink rim to the gingerbread-coated commands scrawled across it. I couldn't rip it down, I knew, but there had to be *something* I could do.

With one swipe of my left forearm I erased the words on the beauty board. It was so easy. What had I expected—a snapping alligator to attack? Yeah, maybe. Grabbing the dry-erase pen dangling from a pink, coiled cord, I wrote the silliest thing I could think of on Dijon's board. I made sure to add lots of goofy *X*'s and *O*'s.

Hey, Peeps!
Try Rebel lip balm:
Firefly!
XOXOXO

Dijon would be the first to see it in the morning and quickly erase it (or, more likely, order Venice to do it for her). That was okay. Somebody—I mean, Nobody— needed to send a message to Her Fabulousness that we weren't afraid of her anymore. Except I hadn't signed my name, which, I suppose, sent a message that I *was* afraid.

Why was it that even as one part of me stood up to her, another part of me always found a way to turn back into mist?

Seventeen

I placed the pink envelope flat on the center of the desk with her name facing up. On top of the envelope I balanced a trio of mango lollipops, with an orange ribbon tied around their sticks. It was a peace offering. A friendship offering. Adair loved lollipops. Mango was her favorite.

Hopping into my seat across the aisle from Adair's, I got out my leadership notebook and started skimming my notes. It was Friday—our last chance to give our project presentation. We could *not* screw it up. Glancing over my shoulder, I saw that Renata's desk was empty. My stomach did a pretzel twist, but there was still five minutes until the first bell. Plenty of time.

Venice and Truffle came into class wearing their tiaras. Dijon wasn't with them. She wasn't at her desk, either. Both girls took their seats, got out their phones, and began texting.

Opening my sketchbook, I pretended to make last-minute changes to the mural design when what I was really doing was keeping an eye on the door for Adair and Renata. A few seconds after the first bell rang, Adair appeared. When she saw the tepee of lollipops, she slowly scanned the room before cautiously sliding into her seat. Adair moved the lollipops to one side, like they were tiny bombs. She opened the envelope and gently slid out the card. On the front of the card was a photo of a cuddly, white kitten, surrounded by baskets brimming with strawberries, blueberries, and raspberries. When you opened the card, it said: "I sure am berry sorry."

Sappy, I knew, but they didn't exactly have an I'm an Idiot section at Hallmark.

Beneath the printed words, I'd written:

Dear Adair,

I'm sorry I thought you told Dijon about our mural. You are one of my best friends, and I

never, ever, ever, EVER want that to change.
Hope you like the lollipops!

Love,
Hot Coco
(Your favorite drink, remember?)

PS I've got a new tongue-twister for you. Try
saying this one three times fast: Liezel licks lime
lollipops! ☺

When Adair lifted her eyes from the card, I was the first thing she saw. And those few seconds when I didn't know which way it was going to go, if her gaze would turn to stone or melt into forgiveness, was complete agony.

When, at last, her eyes crinkled, I was free to breathe.

"I'm sorry too," she said softly, turning the bunch of lollipops over in her hand. "Thanks, Coco."

Something lightly ricocheted off my spine. On the floor, by my foot, a Junior Mint was spinning to a stop.

"Guess who?" Adair tipped her head toward the back of the room.

When I turned, Breck was deeply studying some-thing on the ceiling. He was also holding a Junior Mints box. Not exactly the brightest criminal in the eighth grade. Unless, of course, he wanted to get caught . . .

I was starting to sound like Adair.

The tardy bell rang.

"Coco!" Adair's voice was laced with panic. "Where's Renata?"

My head snapped around. Renata's seat was still empty. I felt the life drain from me. After our talk in the practice room, after her makeover at Fawn's house, after everything we had done to boost her self-esteem, it wasn't enough.

I laid my cheek against the cool, smooth desktop.

From my angle I had a clear view of Venice. She'd put her phone away. Now she was staring into a round mirror propped against her notebook, brushing black mascara onto her lashes. "Looks like you're one team member short, Cuckoo," said Venice. "That's going to drop your grade for—"

My head still on my desk, I waited for her to finish. But Venice was a statue, her hand frozen in midstroke. I realized then the whole classroom had gone quiet. Very quiet. Horror-movie quiet.

Someone was touching my left shoulder. Adair, probably.

Lifting my head, I saw why the room had gone deathly still. Shock will do that to you—paralyze you. And things at Big Mess didn't get any more shocking than this.

Raccoon eyes bulging, Venice gasped. "Is that—?"

"Renata Piñata?" finished Truffle.

Wearing Fawn's pale-green peasant top with bell sleeves, a short mossy-green suede skirt with matching tights, and dark-brown leather boots, Renata Zickelfoos glided down our row. Shiny, reddish-brown hair fell to her shoulders, held back by a dainty mother-of-pearl barrette. Her forehead was softened by a fringe of wispy bangs. *My* bangs. I sat up to my full height. Renata's face glowed—quite a feat given she was walking beneath the row of fluorescent lights that always flickered.

"She looks beautiful," said Adair.

"She looks like the forest," I said.

Already the seaweed hair, enormous sleeves, and wool scarf were fading from my head. The only physical remnant of the old Renata was her red plastic glasses. I was glad she'd kept them. Not that she'd had much choice. The girl still had to see. But I hoped she wasn't in too much of a rush to replace them with new frames. The two red rectangles were a reminder that all we'd really done was a bit of hocus-pocus. It was Renata who was changing—from the inside out.

When Renata saw me, her glistening pink lips turned up and a tiny dimple appeared on each side of her mouth. Honey eyes filled with pride looked into mine. As Renata passed my desk, I felt a breeze. It felt cool and fresh and wonderful.

Parker Silberhagen let out a whistle from the back of the class, and the spell was broken. Almost everyone, except the Somebodies, rushed Renata, to talk to her and touch her and be sure she was, in fact, real. It was too bad Dijon wasn't here. But Venice was holding out her phone and snapping pictures like mad, so I figured it was only a matter of seconds before Her Fabulousness got the news flash.

When Mr. Tanori called us up for our presentation, Renata did not hesitate. In fact, although she sat behind us, she was the first one out of our group to make it to the front of the room. I could hear her humming as she whizzed past my desk.

"What is she doing?" whispered Adair.

"Relaxing."

Adair looked bewildered.

"How are you feeling?" I asked Renata as she prepared to face the class.

"Like I can really do this," she said, wiggling her hands and feet. "Who should be my friendly face in the audience?

"Breck," I said, without thinking.

Renata gave me a satisfied nod, the kind of nod you give when you know something the other person doesn't think you know and maybe doesn't want to acknowledge knowing herself. You know? In short, there was far too much knowing in that nod.

Renata spun on her heel, and before I could even send one positive thought in her direction, she started talking. "Hi, everyone. Sorry about what happened the other day. I got a little nervous, but I'm okay now. So I'm just going to be honest and tell you that we had the same idea as another group. We want to paint the ugly wall in the cafeteria too."

Venice let out an injured puppy squeal.

"But that really shouldn't surprise anyone," Renata continued, with a brief glance in Venice's direction, "because it's not exactly a school secret that we need to paint the wall. I sit by it at lunch, and practically every day someone walks by and says how gross it is—the wall, I mean, not my lunch. How many of you have said that to your friends?"

I flung my hand into the air. So did Adair. Pretty soon, the whole class, except for Venice and Truffle, had their hands up, which was crazy because they'd claimed painting the wall was *their* idea.

"Thanks," said Renata, motioning for everyone to put down their hands. "There *is* one thing that makes our idea different from the other group. It's Coco's design. See for yourself." Stepping out of the way, she smiled at me. I gave her a thumbs-up. She had done her part perfectly. And she hadn't lisped. Not even once.

As I opened my sketchbook, I touched the little silk pouch dangling from the zipper. If my mother's talisman held any luck at all, I needed it now. I turned the book toward the class, held it high, and explained the inspiration behind my design and how I'd done it.

"Coco, please walk up and down the aisles so everyone can get a good view of your drawing," Mr. Tanori instructed.

Yes! I felt a tingle go through me. He hadn't let Dijon walk around the room with her alien dog picture. While I circled the room, Adair started her portion of the talk.

"We figure it will take about a month to paint the mural if we work before and after school, maybe less, if some of Mrs. Wyndham's art students help us. We've arranged it so they'll be able to earn extra credit. . . ."

When I paused at Truffle's desk, she barely glanced at my sketch before turning back to doodling flowers in her own notebook. Venice held out her cell phone and snapped a photo of my design. To send to her queen, no doubt.

Edging toward Breck's desk, I felt the hair on my arms stand up. I told myself it was only static electricity. When I stopped at his desk, my heart was thumping uncontrollably against my rib cage. I didn't have a silly excuse for that.

Dipping my head, I held out my sketchbook.

"I owe you a big apology."

"Me?" I let out a squirrely giggle. Idiot. How old was I, nine? "You mean, for the Junior Mints?"

"No." He picked at his thumbnail. "For, uh . . . telling Dijon about your idea."

"You? *You* stole our idea?"

"I heard Renata say we ought to paint the orange wall in the cafeteria and . . . I don't know. . . . When I joined Dijon's group, everyone was throwing out ideas in the brainstorm session, and Mr. Tanori was standing right behind us, and I couldn't think of anything else to say . . . so I . . . I just blurted out . . ."

"The wall."

"I didn't think she'd choose it. I mean, it's not like Dijon ever listens to anybody else anyway. Who knew this would be the one time?" He grimaced. "Sorry."

I appreciated his confession. Breck could have kept his mouth shut, and I would never have known he was our idea thief. Of course, now I felt even worse about blaming Adair. "It's okay," I said to him.

Breck spent a lot of time inspecting my design. I spent a lot of time fidgeting while he inspected my design. Finally, he said, "This is really good."

"Thanks. We still won't beat your group."

He made his eyebrows dance. "You never know."

"Come on, let the rest of us see it," said Parker, leaning out from behind Breck.

I had to move on.

When we finished our presentation, we got some decent applause from the class. I was not fooled. This would not have happened, I knew, if Her Fabulousness had been in class.

"Thank you, Renata, Coco, and Adair," said Mr. Tanori. "I'll give you your written evaluations next week." He was smiling, so I was pretty certain we'd done well. "Class, you've now heard all of the PTA project ideas. It's time to vote."

Now?

"Now?" squealed Venice.

Mr. Tanori picked up some strips of paper off his desk. "Take one ballot and pass the rest back. Use a pen to mark your ballot. Vote for one idea only, please. If you vote for more than one, your ballot will not count. Parker, what are you holding?"

"This? A pencil."

"And what do you need to vote?"

"Uh . . . a pen?"

"Correct."

Venice popped out of her seat so fast, her tiara nearly fell off. "But Mr. Tanori, Dijon's not here."

"Then she doesn't get to vote."

That's when Venice said something I'd never heard a Somebody utter before. In all likelihood, it may have *never* been uttered by a Somebody in the entire history of Big Mess. Pounding her fist against the side of her desk, Venice Wasserman, senior member of the Royal Court and first runner-up to the Her Fabulousness title, shouted, "That's not fair!"

And all the peasants throughout the kingdom of Big Mess shouted, "Hooray!"

Well, not really, but we were sure thinking it.

Eighteen

Maybe it was Dijon's absence. Maybe it was Renata's transformation. Maybe it was my design. Or maybe it was a little bit of each of these things that, when rolled up tightly together, created one big cinnamon roll of a miracle. I don't know how to explain it. I only know it happened right in front of me. After we voted, Mr. Tanori counted the ballots and wrote the three top groups on the whiteboard:

Renata Zickelfoos's group: 17 votes

Dijon Randle's group: 7 votes

Cord Nagel's group: 3 votes

As soon as we knew the results, and it was safe to take out my phone, I texted my dad: WE WON!!!!

It was a historical moment. The Nobodies had done the impossible. We had beat the Somebodies! Plus, my faces were going up on the wall in the Big Mess cafeteria. All we had to do was make our presentation in front of the PTA on Monday night to get approval, and it would be official!

I ran as fast as I could to second period, catching up with Fawn as she was opening the door to the girls' locker room. "Renata . . . good job . . . my design . . . class vote . . . and we . . . and we . . ."

Fawn spit out the translation. "Renata did a good job on her presentation and you showed everybody your design and the class took a vote and you . . . and you . . . what?"

My lungs begging for air, I held up my index finger.

"One?"

I nodded vigorously.

She tipped her head. "One what?"

"She means they *won*," said Cadence Steele from behind her.

"You won?"

Another quick nod.

"Oh my God, you won!" Fawn threw her arms around me.

Our celebration was a short one. We had to dress for PE. You didn't want to waste a second getting ready in Coach Notting's class. Sometimes she'd blow her whistle early, and you'd be half-dressed, hobbling like mad, one shoe on and one shoe off, to get into line before she could make a check mark on her clipboard.

"Did you guys see Renata Zickelfoos?" asked Cadence. She was getting dressed on the other side of me.

"What's wrong with her?" called Madysen Prestwick from the far end of the row. Madysen was the best softball player in school, and one of the few Sortabodies willing to talk to a Nobody now and then (particularly when Dijon wasn't around, like today).

"Not one thing," said Cadence. "That's just it. She looks like a completely different girl."

"I heard she got a makeover at the mall," said Nari Okada, Madysen's best friend and the second best softball player at Big Mess.

"I heard she got her hair done at that new salon on Bridgeport," said Cadence.

"You mean Monique's Chic Boutique," said Madysen. "I've been dying to go there."

"It's *très* expensive," said Nari. "Dijon says they are the best."

I stole a glance at Fawn. She could hardly contain her grin. I was having the same trouble. What would they say if they knew Renata's clothes were from Fawn's closet and her hair was courtesy of Coco's Chic Boutique?

Cadence leaned back on the bench we shared. "Fawn, she's wearing a top that looks like one you have."

Fawn did a good job of pretending to be surprised. "Really?"

"Except it's a lighter green, and the sleeves are different. It's really cute."

"I heard she got nominated for fall court," said Fawn.

"I'd vote for her," said Nari. She lowered her voice to say, "I get so tired of the same people winning over and over again."

Several girls, including me, nodded.

"Does anyone know what lunch Renata has?" asked Madysen.

"Second," I said, pulling my T-shirt over my head. Our colors at Big Mess were silver and green with black accents, so did they let us wear a nice shade of gray or black for our PE uniforms? Of course not. We had to wear emerald green T-shirts and matching shorts. We looked like a bunch of tree frogs.

"Madysen, Cadence, and I have second lunch too," said Nari. "We'll look for her."

Were they serious? Sortabodies Madysen, Cadence, and Nari would *look* for Renata in second lunch. This was incredible! Even though I knew it might make me late for class, I had to text Renata: BIG NEWS! CADENCE, MADYSEN, AND NARI WANT TO EAT WITH U!

"Don't forget I'll be late for lunch today," Madysen said to her best friend. "Save me a spot, okay?"

"Right, you've got that emergency thing."

"What emergency thing?" asked Cadence.

"The band we hired for the fall dance canceled," said Madysen. "I guess they broke up or got arrested or something. I don't know. Now we've got two weeks to find another band or Dr. Adams is going to cancel the dance. All the other schools have booked the good bands already. I don't know what we're going to do."

Fawn and I straightened up so fast, we banged heads. "Avalanche!" we shouted.

Shrinking, Madysen covered her head. "Where?"

"Not where. What." I tugged on the outside pocket of my backpack. *Please let Liezel's CD be there. Yes!* "It's Liezel Sheppard's band. They're fantastic. Listen for yourself," I said, handing the jewel case to Fawn to pass to Madysen. "I heard they sent in a CD to be considered for the dance, but didn't get chosen."

Turning the CD over in her hand, Madysen twisted her lips. "Really? Dijon said her brother's band was the only one available in our price range, so we went with them without hearing them play first. Big mistake. I heard their CD last week. They're called Make It Strike. They should have been called Make It Stop."

Everybody laughed.

Thweeeeeeeet.

It was Coach Notting's whistle.

"She's two minutes early," squeaked Cadence.

Cramming my foot into my tennis shoe, I raced for the door. With Dijon gone, I was between Fawn and Cadence in the line. I had barely finished tying my shoes when the tardy whistle blew.

Thweeeeeeeet.

"I see we're a bunch of slugs today!" roared Coach Notting, stopwatch in hand. The black velour track-suit, with two thick, yellow stripes down the sides of her arms and legs, made her look like a wasp. Soon after Coach Notting started her inspection, she gave Nobodies Jolie Cartwright and Mave Javilowsky check marks. I didn't see why. They looked fine to me. The closer she came to me, the colder my hands and feet got. I'd heard the air temperature near Coach Notting was seven degrees colder than anywhere else in school. Fawn said one of the science classes did a weather experiment on her last year. She makes her own fog. True story.

Coach Notting gazed at Fawn's magenta-striped hair and clicked her tongue. Fawn put up a self-conscious hand to try to cover the stripe.

When it was my turn, I made sure to not look directly into Coach Notting's eyes. Instead, I stared at my shoes, which, I was proud to say, were both tied with neat bows. From head to toe, I was the epitome of tree-frog perfection.

Keep moving, Coach Notting. Nothing to see here. Just one more step. Take one more step . . .

"Sherwood!"

I jumped.

"What's wrong with your shirt?"

I pulled on the hem of my T-shirt, madly searching for a spot of dirt or a stain. I didn't see a thing, not even a speck of lint. "I don't—"

"It's faded."

"But—"

"Look at Ralston's and Steele's shirts. They're not faded. Yours is faded. What's the problem?"

I looked at Fawn's shirt. It *was* a deeper green than mine. So was Cadence's.

"Uh . . . I don't know . . . My dad usually washes it and it comes out fine. He must have made a mistake—"

"Mistakes, Sherwood, are like dandelions. You can't get rid of them unless you're willing to dig out the roots."

"Um . . . sorry?" I winced.

Now I was going to get the "apologies are like traffic lights" simile. Or were apologies like belly buttons? I couldn't remember.

Coach Notting tapped her pen against her clipboard. But she didn't toss out a simile or make a check mark. "From now on, tell him to wash it in *cold* water."

"Okay."

Coach Notting started to move past me. Maybe she was in a good mood. Maybe she was going to let me off this time. Maybe I was about to catch a break.

"And get a new shirt by Monday," barked the coach. "We are Briar Green, not Briar Mint."

Swish! The pen made a stroke on her aluminum clipboard.

Stocklifter did a poor job of muffling a snort. It echoed through the locker room. I didn't care. My artwork was going up on the big wall in the cafeteria, and nothing, not taunts from the Royal Court or Coach Notting's Clipboard of Doom, was going to spoil it.

On the way to third period I checked my messages.

I had a text from Renata: THEY WANT 2 EAT WITH ME? U SURE?

I wondered if Renata had ever eaten lunch with someone who wasn't an adult.

I texted back: YEP. ☺

She answered right away: WHAT DO I DO?

My fingers flew.

BE U.

HAVE FUN.

LOOK UP.

Nineteen

On Saturday morning Aunt Iona took me to Talbert's Athletic Supply to buy a new green T-shirt for PE class. I told her I needed some new socks, too, so we swung by the mall. I showed her a pair of adorable pink socks with little ice-cream cones, cupcakes, and slices of cheesecake. "Aren't these great? Fawn has this exact pair."

"I don't know, Coco." My aunt made a face. "They won't go with anything."

"They're not supposed to go with anything. That's the point. They're supposed to be fun."

"This is what you need." She held up a bag crammed full of boring, white crew socks. "Plus, they're much more durable than those thin socks. They'll never wear out."

Just what I needed: eternal socks.

She tossed two bags at me. "You'll thank me later."

I doubted that.

I may not have gotten the socks I wanted, but my aunt did buy me a silver, star-shaped compact with four shades of blush. By the time we got to Costco for our usual Saturday afternoon store d'oeuvres, my depression had lifted. Sort of. It was just the two of us today. Fawn had a family wedding to go to, and Adair didn't tell me why she couldn't make it—probably something cheer related.

Sigh.

My aunt and I had munched our way through bacon quiche, pepperoni pockets, pineapple upside-down cake, and mini hash browns. We were working our way toward the bakery when I saw her.

It had to be a mirage.

Dijon Randle in a Costco?

I blinked several times. It was her, all right. She was with her mother. Mrs. Randle was tall and thin, with dark hair and eyes, like her daughter. A leopard-print blouse floated over a black camisole and black jeans. She was wearing some serious jewelry: a stack of turquoise bracelets on her right wrist and silver hoop earrings big enough for my hamster to jump through. Steering an empty cart, Dijon was following her mother. They were headed straight for us!

Grabbing my aunt's elbow, I tried to make a 180-degree turn. Any other time it would have been easy to slip into the crowd without being seen, but today I was battling an unbeatable force: four-cheese macaroni.

"Yum!" gushed my aunt, inhaling deeply. The smell of bubbling cheese gave her superhuman strength, and she surged forward, dragging me with her. My hip hit the corner of Dijon's cart.

"Ow!"

"Oh, sorry—" Dijon turned. "Coco?"

My first impulse was to run. I would have done it too, had there not been a wall of toilet paper blocking my path.

Dijon steered her cart out of the busy aisle. "You okay?"

Excuse me? Was Her Fabulousness inquiring about *my* well-being? Clearly, there was a rift in time inside the Oak Harbor Costco, because a parallel universe was the only explanation for why a Somebody would show even a smidgen of concern for a Nobody.

My aunt was at my side. "Ah, a friend from school?"

Now, how was I supposed to answer that?

"Uh . . . this is Dijon Randle. Dijon, this is my aunt, Iona Sherwood."

"Nice to meet you." Dijon seemed sincere. Almost shy. I didn't like this at all. What was she trying to pull?

"My pleasure. You should try the mac and cheese. It's heaven." Aunt Iona offered Dijon the sample she had brought for me. It figured.

Dijon looked longingly at the noodles swimming in thick, golden sauce topped with a crunchy parmesan crust.

"Dijon!" Mrs. Randle was stalking toward us. "You're supposed to stay close. I told you this place is a zoo— Oh." She noticed us.

"Mom, this is Coco Sherwood," said Dijon, so softly it was practically inaudible. "And her aunt."

"Hello," clipped Mrs. Randle, limply shaking the hand my aunt put out. She looked around in that way you do when you hope something better will come along to rescue you—and soon. "Wait a minute, did you say Coco?"

Dijon winced. It was quick, but it was there.

Mrs. Randle peered down at her daughter. "Is this the one?"

Dijon tipped her chin down.

Mrs. Randle stroked one of her big earrings. "You must be so proud of your daughter."

"Yes, I am." Iona did not correct her.

"How many children get their artwork displayed on such a grand scale?"

"Oh, you mean about the PTA improvement project." Aunt Iona put her arm around my waist. "Isn't that something? The girls worked awfully hard on their proposal. . . ." Mrs. Randle's face was getting redder, but my aunt didn't notice. She kept on talking. "And we couldn't be more excited about the mural."

"It's not yet official," I hurried to say, "but Mr. Tanori said the PTA is sure to approve it at the board meeting."

"Did he?" Mrs. Randle tapped a long, turquoise fingernail against her rosy chin.

Suddenly the corner of the toilet paper wall collapsed. I may have been the cause. My aunt and I rushed to pick up about a dozen twenty-roll packs and restack them. Mrs. Randle and Dijon made no move to help us. Instead, Mrs. Randle took control of the cart from her daughter and began to move away. "Nice to have met you, Kiki."

"Coco," corrected Dijon.

Mrs. Randle gave an impatient flick of the wrist, and her bracelets clinked. We watched the two of them stroll away. Neither of them looked back.

A fog of doom settled over me. Even staying the night with my aunt and playing with her Westie terrier, Gatsby, which *always* cheered me up, couldn't seem to get it to lift. I got into bed around ten o'clock, and instead of going right to sleep, decided to sketch Gatsby, who was asleep beside me. Before turning out the light, I slid my mother's portrait from its pocket in the back of my book. "Our idea won," I told her, "so why am I so jumpy? I can't help feeling like something is going to mess it up. Am I just being paranoid?"

This was so frustrating. I was talking to a piece of paper. Again. Always.

I threw the covers off my legs, found my phone, and started to text my mom. Only a few words in, I stopped. It would take her weeks, maybe months, to reply. I couldn't wait that long. I needed to hear her voice. Now. I didn't know what time it was in Taiwan, and I didn't care. I found her name in my contact list and pressed the button before I could change my mind. Her phone rang three times. Shoot! I was going to voice mail.

After the fourth ring, nothing happened. No more rings. No voice mail. Then, something strange.

"Hello?"

"Mom?" My throat closed. "Is that you?"

"Coco?"

"Yes, yes!" I couldn't believe it. It was her. It was really her!

The last time we had spoken was a few days after my dad and I moved to Oak Harbor last spring. I had called to give her our new address. We had talked for exactly two minutes and fifty-two seconds before she said she had to go. I had timed it.

"How are you, honey?" she asked. "Is everything okay?"

"Everything's great."

"I can barely hear you. Did you get your package?"

"Yes, thanks. I put the charm on my sketchbook and—"

"Good," she jumped in. She said something else, but static garbled it.

"Mom, I . . . uh . . . miss you."

She was cutting in and out. "What?"

"*I miss you*. I've been wanting to talk to you."

"Oh. Okay."

"See, there's this project at school. The class voted,

and my art design won, but now I'm freaked that this really popular girl named Dijon is going to ruin it for me. She's mad that her design didn't win, and I just know that she's going to do something to sabotage me before the PTA can approve—"

"Coco, I can't hear. . . . I'm about to get on a boat. Can I call you back?"

Did she say a boat?

"Uh, yeah . . . sure. When?"

"Well, let's see . . . about fifteen hours ahead . . . tomorrow?"

"Tomorrow? Is that your tomorrow or my tomorrow?"

"What? I'm sorry . . . hear you. I'll call you . . . I can. Hugs, baby."

She was gone.

I sat on the edge of the bed, staring at my phone. My mother wasn't going to call me back. Not tomorrow her time. Or my time. Or any time. Some gripping experience, like zip-lining across a giant canyon or cooking octopus with a world-class chef, would come up, and she would "forget." In a week or so, she might send me a text. And in about six months I would get something nice in the mail. The text would be short and unapologetic. The something nice would be unique and completely wrong for me.

What was I thinking? I shouldn't have called her. Why had I expected that this time would be different? Someday I would tell her how much it hurt when she "forgot" me. Someday I would tell her a mother isn't supposed to leave her daughter behind, even to be a famous travel writer. But she'd have to stay on the phone longer than three minutes for me to say all that, wouldn't she?

Suddenly I was dead tired.

"You want anything to drink before bed?" My aunt stood in the doorway.

"No." I tossed my phone on the nightstand.

"I've been thinking about what you said today."

"What did I say?" And more important, why was she thinking about it?

"About the socks. You said they weren't supposed to go with anything." She came toward me. "I was thinking I could probably use a little more fun in my life. How about we go buy some wild socks this week?"

I knew what was going on. Aunt Iona was a family counselor. And an expert eavesdropper. She had overheard my conversation with my mother and was doing what therapists call overcompensating. That was okay with me. I could use someone who cared enough to interfere in my life about now.

I smiled. "I'm available all week, except Monday."

"It's a date," she said, dropping a kiss on my forehead. "Good night, Amazing Artist."

"Good night, Even More Amazing Aunt." I crawled into bed.

She switched off the light, started to leave, then turned back. "Oh, and about that mustard girl?"

I giggled under the covers. "Dijon."

"Yeah. I wouldn't worry about her. I saw the look on her face today. That girl is scared of you."

I started to say, "I don't think so," but when I lifted my head, Iona was gone.

It was kind of her to say that, but my aunt didn't know Dijon the way I did. Her Fabulousness wasn't frightened of anybody, least of all me. I pulled the blanket up under my chin and stared at the ceiling. Still, we *had* won the contest in leadership class, and that might have threatened her. A little. To be on the safe side, I vowed to stay out of the way of Her Fabulousness and the Royal Court until *after* the PTA meeting. It was two days away, and only one of those days was a school day, so how hard could it be?

My plan would have worked perfectly, too, had it not been for one tiny hitch.

On Monday morning I got on my bus with my new PE T-shirt in my backpack. I wasn't about to give Coach Notting another opportunity to "simile" me. I could already hear her shouting in my head. "You know, Sherwood, forgetting things is like upchucking clam chowder. You only want to do it once."

Ugh.

Three stops later Liezel got on the bus.

"I'll bet you can't guess what happened to me this weekend," she squealed, sliding in beside me. "Not in a million, trillion years."

I bet I could. But I didn't. I let her tell me.

"Madysen Prestwick called. She's the head of the dance committee. They want to hire Avalanche to play at the fall dance!"

"Congrats!"

"I was so excited, I don't think I slept at all last night. You are coming, right?"

"To the dance? I don't know . . ." I rarely went to

school dances. There's an awful lot of "much-ness" at a dance. Too much pressure to dance with someone that was not above your status level but also not below your status level. Too much pretending to be funnier or smarter or happier than you were. Too much warm punch and cheese in a can.

"Please, Coco, you have to come. You *have* to."

I gave in pretty easily. I really *did* want to see her band play live.

"Did you do your math homework?" Liezel asked as we got off the bus.

"Uh-huh."

"Did you figure out that last story problem on integers?"

I fell into step beside her on the sidewalk. "You mean the one about the distance between the top of Mt. Rainier and the bottom of Death Valley?"

On a typical morning at Big Mess it wasn't unusual to see other girls chatting with their friends, talking on their phones, and wexting (you know, walking and texting at the same time). When Liezel and I strolled up the main walkway, the sun was in our faces, and we were discussing our math homework, so I wasn't paying much attention to the other kids moving around us. But by the time we'd reached the shadow of the building, I could tell something wasn't right.

I stopped in the middle of the walkway and turned in a slow, tight circle. In the frosty morning air my breath formed little clouds in front of me. As I realized what was going on, the clouds came faster and faster.

Had I done this?

"We didn't have to do the bonus questions at the end of the chapter, did we?" asked Liezel, still not seeing what I was seeing.

Évian and Venice were coming toward us. Venice was chewing a thick wad of gum. *Snap. Snap. Snap.*

"Oh no!"

I *had* done this.

Liezel moaned. "I knew I should have done the bonus questions."

Venice blew a blue bubble at me, then popped it.

Bang!

"What are you staring at, Cuckoo?" she asked.

I said the first thing that came to my mind. I said, "Fish."

Venice tipped her head in wonder, but it was the only thought going through my head. Their lips glow-ing bright yellow, Venice and Évian reminded me of a pair of tropical tang fish!

"Coco?" Liezel was nudging me. "What in the world *is* that?"

"That," I answered weakly, "is Firefly lip gloss."

Twenty

I felt dizzy. And cold. And hot. And did I say dizzy?

"I never meant for *this* to happen," I said to myself, rushing past Venice and Évian. "She was the only one who was supposed to see the board."

"Who?" asked Liezel.

"Dijon." I flung open the door.

"Oh my God!" Liezel was on my heels. "You touched the sacred beauty board while I was acting as our lookout, didn't you?"

"How was I supposed to know she was going to be absent?"

"This is brilliant!" Liezel laughed. "Just look at everybody."

That's what I was trying *not* to do. I flung my hoodie over my head and raced down the hallway.

"Hi," said seventh grader Brie Alvarez, her lips shining like a couple of glow sticks at midnight.

"Hi," we said.

"Unreal," said Liezel, her head swiveling. "They're all wearing some ridiculous lip gloss because a popular girl told them to."

"They *thought* a popular girl told them to," I corrected.

Apparently, no one, not even a Somebody, had dared to question Dijon's board. Instead, with Her Fabulousness gone on Friday, they'd done as they'd always done: They had obeyed. Over the weekend, hundreds of middle-school girls had raced to the mall to purchase—and were now proudly wearing—the worst lip gloss in the history of girlkind. When they found out the truth, they were going to be shattered! Nobodies were fragile creatures. You couldn't always see the cracks—they might be hidden under a bulky coat or behind a tenor saxophone case—but they were there. One little tap in the wrong spot, and a person could fracture into a million pieces. And all because I thought it would be funny to get back at Dijon. How could I have been so thoughtless?

"I won't tell," said Liezel as we turned the corner to B wing. "Nobody ever has to know you did it, if that's what you're worried about. Besides, no one with an ounce of common sense takes that whole beauty board stuff—"

Fawn was standing in front of our locker. She was not alone. Adair was there too, looking like she ought to be swimming in the tropical tank at the aquarium with Venice and Évian.

"Seriously," finished Liezel.

Fawn gestured to Adair as we approached. "Look, our very own garden solar gnome."

"Clever," said Adair. She held the tube of lip gloss out to Liezel. "Want to try some?"

"No, thanks," said Liezel, putting her books in our locker. "It's a little bright for me."

"A little?" Fawn rubbed her eyes. "I'm starting to see spots."

"Well, I like it," announced Adair.

"Only because Her Fabulousness told you to," I said.

"That's not true."

"How come when I told you about Firefly lip gloss, you said, 'Ick to the hundredth power'?"

"Well, that was . . . before." Adair's mouth formed a pouty O, making her look more like a fish than ever. "And I asked you to stop calling Dijon names."

"Why don't you ever tell Venice to quit calling me Cuckoo or Liezel Weasel?"

Adair ignored me, pretending to be deeply engrossed in a chipped fingernail.

We heard the *clitter-clap*, *clitter-clap* of heels against white-and-green-speckled tiles. Turning, I found myself face-to-face with Dijon. Venice, Évian, and Stocklifter flanked her. Venice and Évian were furiously wiping gloss from their lips with tissues. Clearly, Dijon had informed them of the security breach at the beauty board.

Dijon's eyes drilled into me. "I know what you did, Coco Sherwood. What gives you the right to touch other people's stuff?"

I wanted to argue with her, to say what I had done was not anywhere near as bad as what she had done to Fawn. But I remembered my plan to get through the day and the PTA meeting tonight without any royal drama. "Sorry, Dijon," I said as sincerely as possible. "I shouldn't have written on your beauty board."

"You?" the entire circle of girls, including Dijon, said simultaneously.

Fawn's thumb motioned to Adair. "*You* did this?"

I lifted a shoulder.

"I wasn't talking about the board," said Dijon. "I meant—"

"Oh, you mean, the stinky gym sock and sauerkraut under your locker," I squeaked. "Sorry about that, too."

Dijon's mouth fell open.

"*That* was you!" shrieked Venice, flicking her tissue at me. "You owe me for, like, five cans of Glade, Cuckoo."

"She does not," said Liezel, muscling her way between Venice and Stocklifter. "Dijon bullied Fawn out of her own locker. She started it."

"She did not," spat Stocklifter.

"Did, too!" I cried.

"You shut up!" shot Venice.

"*You* shut up," Liezel fired at Venice.

"She yelled first," snapped Venice, pointing at me, which set off a chain reaction of accusations about who started what and when. Stock, Venice, and Évian were shouting at Fawn, Liezel, and me, who were, naturally, shouting right back.

"Quiet!"

We froze at Dijon's scream.

"Is everything okay out here?" Mrs. Dawkins stuck her head out of the library.

All eight of us nodded.

"Please keep it down, girls. I don't want to have to come out here again." The librarian turned away.

Putting her hands out in front of her, Dijon took a long, deep breath. "I wasn't talking about the beauty board or the smelly locker, though we *will* be discussing these things later." She whirled to face me. "I was talking about my tiara."

I tipped my head. "What about it?"

"As if you didn't know."

I didn't. "What?"

"It's missing."

"Missing?"

"It was in my locker last Friday, and now it's not. Évian told me she'd seen you'd sneaking around my locker, and with all of the weird smells and everything—"

"You think *I* took *your* tiara?" I couldn't help snorting. "What would I possibly want with that dumb thing?"

Dijon's pretty lips became a thin line. "Look, I'm not going to get you in trouble for stealing it. I just want it back. I *need* to have it back." It was the first time I'd ever heard desperation in Dijon's voice.

A shudder went through me.

"I told you, I don't have it. I didn't take it," I said. "I don't know what else I can say."

"If that's the way you want it, Coco." Dijon stuck her chin up, flung her hair over one shoulder, and pushed past me. The Royal Court was inches behind her.

Clitter-clap, clitter-clap. Clitter-clap, clitter-clap.

The usual heel clicking doubled in speed as the four of them marched in perfect time down the hallway. Dijon did not stop to wave to a Sortabody or even say hello to Mrs. Gisborne and Waffles, who were coming our way.

"Look!" said Liezel. "I think she's going to the principal's office."

When they approached the intersection in the hall, Her Fabulousness and the Royal Court charged straight through the double doors and into the main office.

"I knew it," said Liezel.

"She sure is upset," said Fawn.

I ran a hand through my hair. "And over some fake crown. It's ridiculous. Dijon has too much control here."

"Not anymore," said Liezel with a grin. "Thanks to you, Coco. When word gets out about what you did to her beauty board—"

"People will hate me," I finished.

"No, they won't," said Fawn, reaching into our locker for her math book. "Well, at first they might. But then they'll realize just how silly they've been, following her orders. You'll be a hero."

"Nah," I said shyly. Opening my backpack, I tossed in my leadership notebook. "Hey, everybody, don't forget, voting for fall court starts today at lunch. We need to get as many people as we can to vote for Renata, okay?"

"I'm on it," said Liezel.

"Practically our whole PE class is voting for her," said Fawn, shutting our locker. She spun the dial. "And I've told everyone in orchestra, too."

For the first time in days, I started to relax. Dijon's power was draining away. I could feel it.

"Coco?" Adair's hand was on my arm. "I wasn't supposed to tell anyone. I swore I wouldn't, but I think I'd better now."

"Better what? What are you talking about?"

"Dijon's tiara." Her eyes were filling with tears. She had a streak of Firefly lip gloss on her chin. "It's . . . it's . . ."

"*What?*"

"It's not hers."

Liezel's face was between us. "Well, whose is it?"

"Her mother's."

"Her mother's?" echoed Fawn.

Adair yanked all of her hair over one shoulder and began twisting it. "Yeah, it's the one she wore at her third wedding—her really, *really* expensive third wedding."

I think I understood. "You mean Dijon's fake tiara is . . . is . . . ?" My throat was collapsing.

Nodding rapidly, Adair said what I could not. "It's real. The diamonds are real."

Twenty-One

I could not stop my hands and legs from fidgeting. A human earthquake, I kept knocking stuff off my desk.

The first-period tardy bell had already rung, and Dijon was not in her chair. Venice had swung around and was forehead to forehead with Truffle.

"Here." Adair had picked my pen up off the floor and was trying to give it back. "Will you stop twitching? You didn't do anything wrong."

"Then you believe me?"

Two dimples appeared. "Always."

Her tone, that familiar warmth, wrapped itself around me. It gave me comfort. And hope. Maybe I hadn't lost her to them after all.

"Guess what?" she asked, not wanting or waiting for me to guess. "Our cheerleading uniforms came in. Coach Notting is handing them out at practice today after school. I'm so excited! I'm officially going to be a cheerleader. Did you ever think it would actually happen?"

"Yes," I said. "It's your destiny."

Mr. Tanori took roll, then called for our attention. "Just a reminder, class, tonight Adair, Coco, and Renata will be presenting their mural idea to the PTA for final approval. The meeting starts at seven p.m. I'll be there to introduce them, and if you can make it, please come. I'm sure they'd welcome your support."

That got a "Yow!" from Parker and Breck in the back of the room.

Ten minutes into the period, Dijon showed up. Her face a mask, she handed Mr. Tanori a hall pass and went to her seat. I was relieved. Maybe Dijon had only pretended to have a diamond tiara so she could show off to her Royal Court and impress Adair. Or maybe Adair had misunderstood. Whatever it was, it was over now.

I got down to work, giving my full attention to the assignment sheet Mr. Tanori had given us on cooperation. A few minutes later I was filling in the blanks when my teacher knelt by my desk. "Coco," he whispered. "Mr. Falkner wants to see you in his office." He put a hall pass on my desk. "Immediately."

My eyes went straight for Adair.

She had her hands over her nose and mouth.

"Take all of your things with you to the vice principal's office, in case you aren't finished by the end of the period," instructed my teacher. "You can finish your assignment sheet at home and turn it in tomorrow. And if you don't make it back before the period ends, I'll see you at the meeting tonight."

"O-okay." I started to gather my books. When I stood up, my legs felt like dry twigs. So did my mouth.

The last thing Adair said to me before I went to the office was "Don't worry. It'll be all right."

Mr. Falkner didn't keep me waiting long. "Dijon Randle says a valuable tiara that she had in her locker was—is—missing," he said, sitting in the maroon leather chair behind his desk. "Do you know anything about it?"

"No," I said, clutching my backpack to my chest. I couldn't seem to stop rocking back and forth, and licking my lips. I'm sure it must have made me look totally guilty.

"She says you've been leaving, uh"—he glanced down at a piece of paper—"sauerkraut and other disgusting things in her locker? Is this true?"

"Well, sort of. Not in her locker, exactly. More like, *under* it. It's a long story."

"She says you have her locker combination."

"See, technically, she's supposed to be locker partners with my friend Fawn. You know Fawn Ralston, right? But Dijon kicked Fawn out of the locker on the first day of school, so Fawn had to move in with Liezel and me—"

"Coco." He put up a hand. " Do you know her combination or not?"

I licked my lips for the billionth and first time. "I do."

"Dijon says she put the tiara in her locker last week. She says she has reason to believe you may have taken it."

"I didn't." I shook my head as hard as I could, which probably made me look even more guilty. "I didn't take it."

Mr. Falkner rubbed his chin. "I'm not accusing you of anything. I'm just trying to get to the truth. Although she definitely made a mistake leaving it at school, I'm under a bit of pressure here. It's a pricey item."

"Pricey? How pricey?"

He took a moment. "Three thousand dollars."

"Three. *Thousand*?" If I hadn't grabbed his desk, I would have fallen out of the chair.

"It's made of white gold and diamonds, according to her mother, who is, by the way, the owner of the crown. And given that Mrs. Randle is a key figure in our school community . . ." Mr. Falkner did not finish. He didn't have to. The vice principal wiped his brow. "To be sure we've covered our bases, I'm going to need to look in your backpack, your locker, and your PE locker. You may come along, if you want, while I do this."

"Can I call my dad and tell him what's going on?"

"Certainly. I had planned to call him before we got started, to explain what we're doing."

"Mr. Falkner, I'm not lying."

He gave me a painful grin. "I believe you, Coco. But just—"

"I know. Just to be sure."

Mr. Falkner went through all of my stuff. He didn't find Dijon's tiara. I knew he wouldn't, but it was still nerve-racking. There's always that part of you that wonders if the missing crown will somehow, magically appear when and where you least expect it. When he was finished, Mr. Falkner thanked me for my patience and handed me a hall pass so I could go back to first period. The paper was damp with sweat. I think we were both glad the whole thing was over.

I strolled into leadership class with no expression on my face. I gave Mr. Tanori my wrinkled, sweat-stained pass and took my seat. I felt Dijon's eyes on me. I lifted my head and stared at her. I did not blink or move. She was the first to turn away.

Adair was poking me. "What happened?"

"Nothing."

"You're not in trouble?"

"No."

"Thank God. Are you ready for our presentation tonight?"

"I think so," I said, pretending to buzz saw all of my fingernails.

Adair giggled.

Mr. Tanori was kneeling between our desks. "Adair, Mr. Falkner would like to see you in his office. Go right away, please."

"I'm sure Dijon gave him all of our names," I explained, trying to calm her. "He's just going down the list—you, me, Fawn, and Liezel. That's all. It's super easy. He'll go through your stuff, and then you'll get to come back to class, like I did."

"Super easy," Adair repeated, her long hair falling in front of her face.

The last thing I said to my friend before she left was "Don't worry. It'll be all right."

When the bell rang twenty-five minutes later and Adair still hadn't returned, I tried to shake off my worry. Mr. Falkner had probably finished his inspection so close to the end of first period that he'd let Adair hang out in the main office until the bell.

I was on my way to second period PE when I heard Fawn behind me. "Coco! Wait up!"

I stopped in the middle of the courtyard. "What's the matter?"

"They found . . . Dijon's tiara . . ."

"Thank goodness that drama is over."

"No, it isn't," gasped my friend, terror filling her eyes. "Because they found it in . . . in . . . the worst possible place." Fawn clung to me. "Coco, they found Dijon's tiara in . . . Adair's locker."

Twenty-Two

"You're awfully quiet."

"Sorry." I gazed out the car window at the line of maple trees whooshing past. If I let my eyes go out of focus, the red leaves made a wispy blur trail across my brain.

"You only ate half of your dinner," said Aunt Iona.

"Sorry."

"Coco, you don't have to keep apologizing."

"Sorry."

"I'm sure everything will get sorted out with Adair."

I didn't see how.

The facts were pretty solid. And pretty sordid. Mr. Falkner had discovered the missing diamond tiara at the back of the top shelf of Adair's locker. Shortly after that, the rumors started rocketing through the halls of Big Mess. Adair had been suspended. Adair had been expelled. Adair had been hauled off to jail by Security

Officer Burton. But I knew the truth. Fawn told me Adair had gotten so upset to her stomach, she'd gone home sick before lunch. I also knew my friend was innocent. For one thing, Adair was too honest to ever steal anything from anyone, and for another, she'd devoted her whole existence to trying to be accepted by popular girls like Her Fabulousness and the Royal Court. She would never blow it over some crown—even one worth three thousand dollars. It didn't make any sense. Something else was going on here. But what? Did someone know I had secretly changed the cheer scores? Was she (or he) trying to get back at me by punishing Adair?

I had been calling and texting Adair all afternoon, but she hadn't responded. I understood if she didn't want to come tonight and face everybody. Renata and I could handle the PTA. But I needed to know that one of my best friends was all right. Adair's silence was painful, and the longer it continued, the worse I felt.

When Aunt Iona pulled up to the curb next to the Big Mess cafeteria, the clock on the dashboard read 6:39. I reached behind the driver's seat, feeling for my nylon backpack. "Thanks for the ride."

"I wish I could stay. If I didn't have group—"

"It's okay."

My aunt led a support group for kids of divorce on Monday nights. I had gone to it for a while after my parents had split. It had helped (more than I was willing to admit at the time).

I got out of the car. "Dad said he was coming right from work, so he should be here by the time the meeting starts."

"Call me when you get home. I want to hear all about it."

"Okay."

It was strange, seeing the Big Mess cafeteria at night. It seemed bigger, yet far less threatening than it did during the day when it was divided by social status. A bunch of parents were clustered together near the cashier's area. In the back Mrs. Gisborne was taking the plastic wrap off a tray of sugar cookies. Incredibly, Waffles was almost perfectly straight! On the left side of the stage Miss Grace was placing several chairs around a rectangular table that held four microphones. Next to her, Mr. Tanori was setting up a laptop and the document camera on a smaller table. A large, white screen hung above his head. On the far right side of the stage stood a wooden podium and microphone.

I touched the ugly, orange wall, and a fleck of paint came off on my finger.

Tipping my neck back, I let my eyes travel across the smooth, concrete surface. I could see my faces here. I could see them watching over the future Somebodies and Sortabodies and Nobodies that would come and go from Big Mess. Maybe one day some kid who didn't have anybody to eat with might look at them—really look at them—and feel a little better. A little more worthy. A little more understood. Wouldn't that be something?

It was sixteen minutes to seven. I checked my messages again.

I had a text from Liezel: GOOD LUCK, BGMS ARTIST OF THE YEAR!

And another from Fawn: U R GOING 2 B GREAT!

But nothing from Adair. Where was she? And why wouldn't she talk to me? Panic swelled in my throat. The "what ifs" were back. What if she didn't come to school tonight? Or ever? What if Adair thought I had something to do with planting Dijon's tiara in her locker? With all of my sneaking around, I had certainly given her reason to suspect me. What if I had lost Adair's friendship forever?

Renata was striding across the cafeteria toward me. Wearing Fawn's pale yellow, sleeveless, A-line dress, with a pair of mocha-brown beaded sandals, she looked like springtime. Renata had pulled the sides of her hair back behind her head, leaving wispy waves to frame her face. Renata's mother was with her. I recognized the eyes.

"Hey, Coco," said Renata. "This is my mom."

"Hello," said Mrs. Zickelfoos warmly, taking my hand. "I've heard a lot about you." The way she said it sent a ripple of joy through me.

"Have you seen Adair?" I asked Renata.

She shook her head.

"I'll let you girls get ready," said Mrs. Zickelfoos, squeezing her daughter's hand. "Good luck, honey."

"Thanks, Mom." Renata's squeezed back.

A pang of envy stabbed my heart.

Mrs. Zickelfoos went to take a seat near the window, while Renata and I headed to the front to let Mr. Tanori know we were there. Teachers, parents, and students were starting to stream in. The tables were slowly filling up. Miss Grace placed three signs on the large table on the left side of the stage: PRESIDENT, VICE PRESIDENT, and SECRETARY. I still didn't see my dad. Or Adair.

"Okay, ladies, we are first on the agenda tonight."

Mr. Tanori straightened his red tie with the tiny white polka dots. "Here's how it will work: I will introduce your group. Renata, you will be first. Go on up the stairs and straight to the podium to the right. Turn the microphone on and give your speech to the audience just the way you did in class. Um . . . I mean, the second time." He chuckled. "Be sure and speak up. Coco, when it's your turn to show the design, place your sketch beneath the document camera, and it will be projected onto the big screen. When you're done with your full presentation, there may be some questions from the PTA officers seated onstage to your right. That's normal. Just answer their questions clearly and briefly, and if you get stuck, I'll be down in the front row, ready to help." Mr. Tanori must have seen the fear on our faces, because he rushed to say, "I'm not anticipating any problems, though. So just have fun, okay?" Our teacher glanced around. "Is Adair here?"

"Not yet," I said.

He straightened his tie again. "She is coming, though. . . ."

"She'll be here," Renata said confidently. To me, she whispered, "If she doesn't come, I'll do her part."

"Thanks." It was good to have Renata to lean on.

Renata went into her relaxation routine of humming and wiggling. I set my backpack on the end of the seat and tried not to hyperventilate.

The air-conditioning system above the stage had kicked on, and it was getting chilly. My head was starting to feel tight. And I had to pee. There had to be at least a hundred people in the cafeteria, and they kept coming. What were they all doing here? I guess a lot of people were curious about the design. I saw Dr. Adams, Mr. Falkner, Mrs. Ignazio, Mrs. Dawkins, and several other teachers. There were plenty of kids, too, including Breck and Parker, and most of the students from my leadership class. It was getting noisy.

There was a thump on my back. "She's here," said Renata.

Adair was coming down the window aisle, politely sliding past a group of students blocking the way. She was wearing her denim jacket, a powder-blue top with a splash of glitter around the crew neck, and jeans. She'd left her hair loose. When Adair lifted her head, her eyes were sunken and bloodshot. "Sorry, I'm late."

I latched on to her arm. "I'm glad you came."

"I almost didn't, but . . . this is our project, and I wanted to see it through."

"Are you okay?" asked Renata.

"You mean, considering I'm suspended for two days?"

"What!" we burst.

"That's not fair," said Renata.

"Everyone knows you didn't take Dijon's tiara," I chimed in. "And we're going to prove it, if it takes all year."

Adair sighed. "You can't right every wrong, Coco."

"We can't let Dijon get away with—"

"Let's focus on what we're here for, okay?"

"But, Adair, you can't just give up—"

"Clarke." Coach Notting was coming in through a side door.

What was *she* doing here?

"Hi, Coach."

"I wanted to tell you how sorry I am about—well, you know—and if there's anything I can do. Well, you know."

"Thank you." Adair's voice broke.

The coach patted Adair's arm. "Go get 'em."

Oh. My. God.

Coach Notting was giving comfort to a student? What parallel universe had I fallen into?

As the coach moved off, my eyes locked on to a green-and-white wave headed in our direction. It was

Dijon, Venice, and Truffle. Her Fabulousness and the Royal Court were dressed in identical sweaters. Of course! Coach Notting had handed out the new cheer sweaters today. No wonder Adair was heartbroken. She had gone home sick and hadn't gotten her beloved cheer sweater. Dijon was in the lead, naturally, so I got the best look at her outfit. A silver horizontal zigzag stripe divided her sweater across the chest. The top third of the V-neck was white, and the bottom two-thirds was emerald green. A giant embroidered black-and-silver St. Bernard dog patch was sewn to the center of her chest. On her right shoulder another patch read "Dijon" in thick, fuzzy, green cursive letters. Truffle and Venice had similar patches with their names on them. The trio strolled to their usual table in the middle of the cafeteria.

Adair couldn't take her eyes off them.

"You'll get yours soon," I said.

"No."

"Sure, you will. Tomorrow you'll—"

"No, Coco," she said firmly. "I won't." The tiniest of tears slipped down a pale cheek. "I've been kicked off cheer staff."

"*What?*"

"Coach Notting had no choice. Section Four, paragraph B of the Big Mess Cheerleading Constitution that I signed states 'Cheerleaders are ambassadors of good sportsmanship and spirit. They must abide by all school rules and not behave in an inappropriate, disrespectful, or illegal manner, thereby dishonoring their school and the athletic team or teams they represent.'"

The fact that she could recite the thing by heart did not surprise me. "You didn't dishonor—" I started to say.

"Stealing doesn't exactly promote school spirit."

"Adair, why do I have to keep reminding you? You didn't steal anything."

"I know, but—"

"I don't know what kind of game Dijon is playing here, but it's not going to work. Tomorrow morning we're marching into Dr. Adams's office—"

"Shh. Please. Not here." Adair put a shaky hand to her forehead. She was barely holding it together, and I wasn't helping.

I put my arm around her. "Sorry."

I would not let Adair down. Somehow I would figure out a way to get her back on the squad. I already had a name for it: Operation Restore Adair.

"Dijon, darling!" We heard the clink of bracelets. Clutching a large cardboard tube under a skeletal arm, Mrs. Randle came down the middle row. She handed the tube to her daughter and continued toward us. Flicking a big chandelier earring made of pink crystals over her shoulder, Mrs. Randle paused to shoot Adair a nasty look. Then she climbed the side stairs to the stage and plopped her huge zebra-print purse on the table next to the first metal sign.

Unbelievable!

This couldn't be right. Dijon's mother was president of the Big Mess PTA?

The nightmare continued as we watched Mr. Wasserman (Venice's dad), Mrs. Gisborne, Miss Furdy, and Coach Notting go up the steps and take their seats at the table onstage. These people were the PTA officers—the ones we had to convince to approve our idea! We were dead before we had even begun.

Whoooo. Whooo. Mrs. Randle blew into her microphone to signal it was almost time to start.

People began settling in. The place was packed. My team sat down, Renata on one side of me and Adair on the other. Renata was rubbing her bare arms. It *was* cold. Craning my neck, I caught sight of my dad strolling through the door. He hadn't seen me yet. But at least he was here.

Deep breaths. Deep breaths. Take one thing at a time.

I could hear Renata humming. Strangely enough, it calmed me, too.

I unzipped my backpack and reached inside. My fingers stumbled over my leadership notebook, my day timer, my geography textbook, and two library books. My stomach did a flip. Quickly, I took everything out of my backpack.

But there was no mistake.

Everything was here, except the one thing I needed: my sketchbook.

That was missing.

Twenty-Three

"Did you lose it?" asked Adair.

"Maybe someone stole it," said Renata.

Adair gasped. "I'll bet it was Stocklifter. Remember last year?"

I made another frantic, pointless search of my pack. "I thought I'd stuck it in here, but I must have taken it out, which means"—I let out a teeny cry—"it's in the backseat of my aunt's car. She dropped me off tonight and—"

"Call her!" hissed my friends.

Keeping my head low, I dialed Aunt Iona's cell. No answer. I left a panicked message. I texted her too, even though I knew it was no use. My aunt would have turned off her phone before starting her support group meeting. For the next hour she would be completely out of touch.

"Oh God," squeaked Renata. "We're grilled cheese."

"Not yet, we're not," I said, flipping my leadership notebook to a blank page. "Here's what we're going to do. I'm going to draw as quickly as I can, and the two of you are going to give your presentation as slowly as you can. Got it?"

"Got it," said Renata, wiggling faster.

I wished she would stop bouncing. I *really* had to pee.

"That will never work," said Adair, until it dawned on her it was our only option. "Well, what are you waiting for—draw, Coco. Draw!"

While Mrs. Randle introduced the board members, I drew. While Mr. Tanori told the audience about leadership class, I drew. While Adair and Renata spoke about our idea, I drew. But fifteen minutes wasn't nearly enough time to create a decent design. So when it was my turn, I stepped up to the podium knowing I was about to disappoint all the people who had put their faith in me. I glanced at Mr. Tanori sitting below the stage. I looked over my shoulder at Renata and Adair, standing behind me. Lastly, I gazed out at my father. He was seated next to the orange wall, about three-quarters of the way back. My dad was grinning, which only made me feel worse. All I'd wanted to do was make a difference. Yet all I had truly done was make a mess.

My legs felt like kelp. I had to lean on the podium to stay upright.

"Uh . . . hi, everybody. I'm Coco Sherwood." It's odd hearing your voice being amplified, like watching a bird circle the room and come back to land on your shoulder.

"Go, Coco!" shouted Parker, which got the crowd to snicker.

For once I was grateful for his big mouth. It gave me a minute to fill my lungs. But soon there was silence again, and all eyes were on me. Hundreds of eyes. On me.

I cleared my throat. Steadied my hands. Locked my knees. And gave myself a little pep talk.

This is your moment to show them you are so much more than they think you are. Start, Coco. Just start.

So I did.

"People are always telling us that we aren't supposed to judge others," I said into the microphone. "But let's face it, that's what we do. Right or wrong, we judge people." I tilted my head to look at the board members. I looked into Mrs. Randle's eyes. "Is she beautiful?" I shifted to look at Miss Furdy. "Does she look good in a cheerleading uniform?" This last one was for Coach Notting. Clutching the podium, I took a breath—the deepest, longest breath of my life—and said, strongly and purely, "Is she popular?"

Coach Notting's head snapped around. I felt her gaze burn into me, but I was determined to keep going.

"My mural design is a collage of twenty-two intertwining faces—one face for each year of our school. I hope my artwork will be a reminder—we don't have to be pretty, petite, or popular. We just have to be ourselves." I pushed myself away from the podium. "Some of my faces are content. Some are miserable. Some are thoughtful. Some are thoughtless. Some are hopeful—"

"Yes, we get it, dear," Mrs. Randle's stern voice filled the room. "Let's see the design."

"Well, I . . . I mean, I had meant to . . ." I crumpled the page. I could not show them this. It was a rough outline of a few faces and some winding vines. "I'm sorry," I said, looking helplessly at Mr. Tanori. "I don't have it. I don't have the drawing."

As if feeling my own agony, the microphone screamed. Everyone covered their ears until the feedback died away.

"This is ridiculous," boomed Mrs. Randle. "We can't vote on a design we haven't seen."

Mr. Tanori was bounding up the steps. "Coco, what happened?"

"I left my sketchbook in my aunt's car," I blubbered.

"I didn't realize it until it was too late. I thought I could do a new drawing while everybody was talking, but"—I opened my fist—"there wasn't time."

He rubbed his temple. "Okay, let's see if we can postpone the vote until—"

"Mr. Tanori," clipped Mrs. Randle, "do you have an alternate design?"

My teacher adjusted his tie. "Well, no. We hadn't planned on—"

"I believe my daughter's artwork came in second place, did it not?"

"Yes, but—"

"Why don't we take a look at the alternate mural design." She snapped her fingers. "Dijon, darling!"

All heads swung to the middle of the room. Funny how everyone, even the adults, knew exactly where Dijon was. With her arm curled around the big cardboard tube, Dijon made her way to the stage. Now I understood. Dijon's alien dog poster was inside the tube. Mrs. Randle had planned to shoot down my idea so Dijon could present hers to the PTA—not that she'd needed to. I had done it for her. Beautifully. Perfectly. I had walked right into this trap all by myself.

Flipping her hair back, Dijon pranced up the steps,

as if she had all the time in the world. And didn't she? This was her kingdom, after all.

It was over.

A Nobody now and forever, I surrendered.

I moved back, giving her a path to the podium. What choice did I have?

Her Fabulousness gently set the tube on the floor. Instead of turning toward the audience, however, Dijon faced me. She held out her arm. What was she doing? Was she making fun of us? She had won. Wasn't that enough? No, of course it wasn't. Winning wasn't enough for a Somebody. They needed you to publicly admit you'd lost. They had to make sure everybody heard you confess it. Only then would their victory be complete.

Fingers pressing into my spine made me stumble forward, and I saw something I never thought I'd see. Not here. And certainly not from *her*. In misty blues and greens, peering out from between winding tendrils and leaves, were Liezel's eyes and Fawn's profile and Adair's dimples. They were smaller than I remembered, but they were there—*all* of my faces—staring out at me from, of all places, Dijon's phone.

I couldn't believe it. Her Fabulousness was going to steal my idea and pretend it was her own!

Twenty-Four

Flames tore through my rib cage. I swallowed bitter liquid. I was going to throw up.

I put a hand over my mouth and turned to run. My eyes found Renata's, and, in that instant, I knew I couldn't do it.

I couldn't let it happen.

I couldn't let Her Fabulousness take one more thing away from us. Not again. Not this. If I wanted my wall, I was going to have to stay. And fight every Somebody who got in my way. Even if it meant hurling fish sticks and fruit salad all over the stage.

Ignoring my gurgling stomach, I swung back around. "No," I said, dropping my hand. "No. No. NO!" With each word I grew less afraid. And more visible.

"Why not?" Dijon looked confused. "Don't you want everybody to see your design?"

"Yes, but—"

"Then take it," she said, wiggling her cell phone. "Take it and show them, Coco."

I couldn't move.

So Adair—brave Adair—reached for the phone.

"You okay?" Renata was beside me.

"Give me a sec," I heard myself say, because I needed time to process what had just occurred. So Dijon Randle, Her Fabulousness of the Supreme Royal Court at Big Mess, had come up onstage not to humiliate me, but to *help* me?

She wasn't going to steal my idea, after all?

As I stood motionless, Adair, Renata, Dijon, Mr. Tanori, and Miss Grace buzzed around me. In less than a minute the photograph of my artwork went from Dijon's phone to Mr. Tanori's laptop to the document camera to the big screen.

Poof!

When the design came up on the screen, the audience began to nod and clap.

"How lovely," said Mrs. Gisborne. Waffles tipped slightly as our head counselor looked up at the screen.

"It's quite ethereal, Coco," said Mr. Wasserman.

"Acceptable work, Sherwood," said Coach Notting.

What? No insult? No check mark? Not even a simile?

She must have seen the look on my face, because Coach Notting said quietly, "I'm hardest on those I think have the most potential, Coco."

"Then you must think I could be president."

Tossing her head back, Coach Notting roared with laughter. It wasn't *that* funny.

And did she just call me by my first name?

"I don't mind that you're hard," I said. "Okay, well, sometimes I mind. I just think a teacher should treat everyone equally."

Coach Notting sucked in her lips, and for a moment I thought she might yell at me. Instead, she said, "True."

I saw Dijon heading for the stairs. "Dijon, wait!"

On the third step she turned.

"You forgot your tube," I said.

"Oh yeah," she said, rolling her eyes and coming back for it.

I put my hand on her arm. I didn't know why. "Thank you," I said.

"You're welcome."

I shifted.

So did she.

I felt I should say something else, but I couldn't think what.

"Look, Coco . . ." Turquoise fingernails dug into the cardboard tube. "I . . . uh . . . I know I said some things to your friends . . . and to you . . ." Dijon's head dropped. She looked at her new white cheer tennis shoes with green-and-silver pom-poms attached to the laces. "It's just hard sometimes, you know? You do certain things, and nobody calls you on them, so you push it a little further and a little further, and before you know it . . ."

You've crossed a line.

Neither of us had to say it out loud.

I was beginning to understand. I had been wrong about Big Mess. The Somebodies hadn't taken control of the school. The Nobodies had freely given it to them. And they could take their power back any time they chose. The thing was, with every flippant comment and parade down the hall and beauty board command, Dijon was daring the Nobodies to stand up for themselves. Maybe she was tired of being queen of the kingdom. Maybe it was more pressure than I, or any of us, knew.

"Hey, guys," Renata said. "Mr. Tanori says the board is ready to vote, and he wants us to take our seats." She rubbed the goose bumps from her arms.

"You cold?" asked Adair, already slipping off her denim jacket. "You can borrow my coat. I'm fine."

"Oh, thanks, Adair," said Renata, starting to put her arm in the sleeve. "It's freezing in here—"

"That's it!" I cried so loudly, Renata dropped the coat.

Dijon, Adair, and Renata were staring at me, like I had asked for a second helping of chicken noodle soup.

"What's it?" asked Renata, her eyes enormous. "Did you see a spider?"

"Something much, much better," I said, my heart leaping up into my throat.

I had solved the mystery! I knew how Dijon's crown had ended up in Adair's locker. It was quite simple, really. Grabbing Adair's jacket off the floor, I yanked the left sleeve inside out to show them three numbers written in permanent black marker. "Ta-da!" I yelled.

Adair frowned. "My locker combination?"

"Why is it on your sleeve?" asked Dijon.

"I wrote it there on the first day of school so I wouldn't have to memorize it."

"Oh," said Dijon.

"Oh," said Renata.

Three pairs of eyes blankly stared at it. Then me. Clearly, I was going to have to connect the dots.

"And what happened . . . ?" I prompted, rotating my

free hand to get her to keep thinking. "Remember? A week ago you loaned your jacket to . . ."

Adair's brow furrowed. "Truffle."

I could see she was starting to catch on. "What if when Truffle got kicked out of Dijon's locker, she decided to get even by stealing her tiara?" I asked. "And because she had your jacket, she also had your—"

"Locker combination," finished Renata.

Satisfied, I folded my arms.

We all took a beat to let it sink in.

Then, as if on cue, the four of us screamed, "TRUFFLE!"

Twenty-Five

"When I say 'briar,' you say 'green.'" Adair shook two silver-and-green metallic pom-poms at our section of the bleachers. "Briar!"

"Green!" We stomped our feet, the rolling roar shaking the gym. Liezel stomped a little too hard, and her shoe went flying. Fawn grabbed it a second before Parker, who was sitting behind us, got to it.

"Briar!"

"Green!"

"BRIAR!"

"GREEN!"

Adair and Dijon did side-by-side split jumps, touching their pom-poms to their toes. I got a cramp in my leg just watching them.

Pep rallies. You had to love 'em, if for no other reason than they got you out of sixth period. Sometimes, if you were lucky, you got a bonus, like teachers tossing raw eggs at one another or Dr. Adams getting a chocolate pie in the face. We watched as Adair and the other cheerleaders threw little bags of green-and-white jelly beans into the crowd. Oh yeah, and there were free snacks, too, though you had to really battle for them.

"Don't forget to tell your dad, my mom's going to pick us up after the dance," said Fawn. Adair, Liezel, Renata, and I were spending the night at Fawn's house.

"He knows," I said. "I am supposed to call him when I get to your house, though, so don't let me forget."

Liezel was madly waving at Adair. "I can't believe she's not even aiming for us."

"She's not?" I took off my hoodie and got in proper jelly bean–catching stance, which is basically on your tiptoes, with your arms as high as you can get them.

Adair had only one bag of jelly beans left to chuck.

"Over here!" I shouted.

Adair cocked her arm and pitched the bag in our direction. It had a decent arc to it, exactly what it needed to make it over the rows of kids in front of me. Using my knees as springs, I burst into the air at the exact moment the bag sailed past. My timing was good. The plastic hit my fingers, but as I closed my hand, the bag tumbled past my fingertips. I was certain

I had lost it when, suddenly, another hand reached up from behind me to support mine. We caught the bag. Together.

"Nice catch," said Breck, dropping his hand.

"You too," I said, my cheeks getting warm. I held up the bag of candy. "You want to split them?"

Breck jumped down a row and scooted in between Liezel and me.

Don't think I didn't see the look that passed between Liezel and Fawn when I poured a few jelly beans into Breck's hands, which, by the way, weren't at all what I'd expected. They weren't dirty or crusty or covered with warts. They looked normal. Nice.

"When do you get to start painting the mural?" Breck asked me.

"In a couple of weeks. We have to wait for the scaffolding. Do you want to help?"

"Sure."

"I've never done anything so big before, but Mrs. Wyndham says she'll help me figure out the scale." I popped a jelly bean in my mouth. "I hope when we're all done, everybody likes it."

Looking at his feet, Breck said, in a voice so low I almost missed it, "What's not to like?"

I was glad I didn't miss it.

The cheerleaders had finished catapulting candy into the crowd. Mrs. Gisborne was walking to the microphone at the far end of the gym, where six empty chairs had been placed in a row.

"What's holding Waffles on?" I asked, squinting.

Liezel leaned forward. "Are those yellow daisies?"

"They look like pieces of Swiss cheese?" said Fawn.

"Or mini waffles," said Breck.

That made us laugh.

It seemed only logical that Waffles the wiglet was being held on by waffles, the barrettes.

"Good afternoon, students," said Mrs. Gisborne, trying to juggle her notes and the microphone in the same hand. "I am pleased to announce your nominees for this year's fall court. In alphabetical order, let's welcome Évian James, Stockholm Ingebrittson, Dijon Randle, Venice Wasserman, and Renata Zickelfoos."

Truffle had been nominated for fall court too; however, she'd been disqualified as part of her punishment for stealing Dijon's crown. Fortunately, Truffle had immediately confessed when she'd been confronted with the evidence. She'd also said she hadn't meant to get Adair into trouble. She'd acted out of anger.

Needing a quick place to stash the tiara, she'd found Adair's locker, well, handy. Still, you couldn't overlook the fact that Truffle didn't admit anything until she'd gotten caught, which was pretty slimy. I guess she was afraid of being kicked off the cheer squad. She *should* have been kicked off too, in my opinion. However, her parents made a big stink over it, and even brought in their attorney, so Truffle got to remain a Big Mess cheerleader. Didn't it just figure?

Everybody clapped as the girls came out in a line and stood next to their chairs. Wearing identical cheer outfits, Évian, Stocklifter, Dijon, and Venice looked like quadruplets. But it was Renata who stole the spotlight. She had on a cherry-red T-shirt dress with three-quarter-inch lace sleeves, black sandals, and a chunky, red bracelet. Her reddish-brown hair was pulled back into a sleek, straight ponytail. Renata looked like a high-fashion model!

I nudged Fawn to tell her "good job."

"It was her idea," she said, shrugging. "She wanted to stand out."

Parker let out a whistle. "Go, Renata!"

Renata waved sheepishly to the crowd.

"It's my privilege to announce your princesses and

queen," said Mrs. Gisborne. Behind her, Adair and the cheerleaders stood next to a table with three crowns and three bouquets of white roses. Alan Dwyer was kneeling off to one side, taking photos for the newspaper and yearbook.

I crossed all my fingers and all my toes. Closing my eyes, I prayed with every corpuscle of my being.

Oh please, oh please, oh please, let her win something! She doesn't have to be queen, but let her be a princess.

I opened one eye to discover Liezel and Fawn were doing the same thing.

Mrs. Gisborne opened the envelope. "Your first princess is . . ."

Oh please, oh please, oh please . . .

"Évian James."

My heart slipped. There was only one princess spot left. We applauded as Adair put a crown on Évian's head—a *fake* crown. Cadence handed her a bouquet. Évian seemed surprised—glad, but surprised.

Mrs. Gisborne ripped open the second envelope. "And your other fall princess is . . ."

I rocked back and forth.

Oh please, oh please, oh please . . .

"Renata Zickelfoos."

We leaped into the air, screaming and hugging and stomping and screaming some more! Renata looked like Mrs. Gisborne had just zapped her with a stun gun, but she managed to remain upright long enough for Adair to pin the crown to her head. Renata was crushing her roses to her chest, as if she feared someone might try to take them away.

Don't worry, Renata. They're all yours.

When we'd finished cheering, I had lost most of my hearing and all of my voice. I also noticed that, somehow, my hand was in Breck's hand. I wasn't quite sure how it had happened. But he didn't let go. And so I didn't either. It could work out, a relationship between a Somebody and a Nobody, right?

A few minutes later Dijon was crowned fall queen. Naturally. Some things never change.

But some things do.

I have the evidence to prove it.

There's a photograph hanging in my locker of Dijon, Évian, and Renata standing shoulder to shoulder in the gym, proudly wearing their crowns and holding their white roses. The headline above them reads "Fall Court Reigns Supreme." Next to that photo is a picture of Liezel, singing and playing her guitar at the fall dance.

It's a little out of focus and a little dark, but the look of joy on her face is unmistakable. She was, as Liezel herself is fond of saying, a girl in the clouds. Beneath Liezel is a close-up of Adair at the first football game of the year. She is waving her pom-poms and, if I'm not mistaken, doing that hideous barking cheer that still haunts me in my sleep. That's not the only thing that haunts me. One day I'll tell Adair how she got on cheer staff in the first place. After she's been a cheerleader for a long, long time and I know she'll forgive me, I'll tell her. Someday.

Now whenever anyone insists it's impossible for things to change, I take them on a tour of the kingdom of Big Mess. First, we stop at my locker for a look at my photo collage of miracles. Then we stroll past Dijon's beauty board, which is still up, though the messages are a bit different these days. Finally, we head to the cafeteria to see my faces on the big wall. That usually does the trick.

Poof!

I've been giving that tour a lot lately.

Well, I couldn't very well stop with Renata, could I? Once you've seen row after row after row of nice, neat, never-make-trouble Nobodies, there's no turning back.

Not counting the five of us, there are 127 Nobodies in the eighth grade alone. I know because we stayed up late at Fawn's sleepover counting every single one.

Good thing my dad and I found a house this week. It has a big front porch.

One hundred and twenty-seven Nobodies.

I—we—have a long way to go.

*One who walks in
another's tracks leaves
no footprints.
XXOO*